Strangers

Other Virago Modern Classics
published by The Dial Press

ANTONIA WHITE
Frost in May
The Lost Traveller
The Sugar House
Beyond the Glass

RADCLYFFE HALL
The Unlit Lamp

REBECCA WEST
Harriet Hume
The Judge
The Return of the Soldier

F. TENNYSON JESSE
The Lacquer Lady

SARAH GRAND
The Beth Book

BARBARA COMYNS
The Vet's Daughter

HENRY HANDEL RICHARDSON
The Getting of Wisdom
Maurice Guest

MARY WEBB
Gone to Earth
Precious Bane

EMILY EDEN
The Semi-Attached Couple
& The Semi-Detached House

MARGARET KENNEDY
The Ladies of Lyndon
Together and Apart

MAY SINCLAIR
Mary Olivier: A Life

Antonia White

STRANGERS

With a new Introduction by
Hermione Lee

The Dial Press
New York

To Lyndall Hopkinson

Published by
The Dial Press
1 Dag Hammarskjold Plaza
New York, New York 10017

First published by The Harvill Press 1954
Manufactured in the United States of America
First printing

Library of Congress Cataloging in Publication Data
White, Antonia, 1899–
Strangers.
(A Virago modern classic)
Contents: The key – The moment of truth
(1941) – The house of clouds (1928) – The
saint (1928) – [etc.]
I. Title.   II. Series.
PR6045.H15634S7   1983   823'.912   82-12852
ISBN 0-385-27786-5

Contents

	PAGE
Introduction	i
The Key, a Poem	1
The Moment of Truth (1941)	2
The House of Clouds (1928)	45
The Saint (1928)	67
Aunt Rose's Revenge (1949)	79
The Exile (formerly called The Mystic) (1935)	99
Strangers (1928)	107
The Rich Woman (1943)	119
Sed Tantum Dic Verbo, a Poem	157
Surprise Visit (1964)	160

Acknowledgments

ACKNOWLEDGMENTS are due to the following journals in which the poems and stories originally appeared: *English Review, Horizon, Life and Letters, Harper's Bazaar, Everyman, Week-end Review.*

Publisher's Note

The last story in this Virago Modern Classic edition, "Surprise Visit," originally appeared in the British periodical *Art and Literature* (1964) and is collected here for the first time.

Introduction

The book for which Antonia White is best known, *Frost in May* (1933), is not merely an unusually vivid 'school story' set in a convent. It pits an emergent individual will against a highly formalized discipline of behaviour and thought. There is a clash between Nanda's developing aesthetic sense and the restrictive intellectual authority of the Church ('I don't want poetry and pictures and things to be messages from God, I want them to be complete in themselves'), between her strong emotional needs and the nuns' disapproval of intimate friendships, and between her self-conscious, anxious assimilation of a new faith and the habitual belief of the girls who are born Catholics.

Nanda, a nine-year-old convert when she enters in 1908 and a fourteen-year-old rebel when she leaves, may resist the convent disciplines, but she is mentally concentrated and exercised by them. The three 'sequels' to *Frost in May*, written in the early Fifties, show the Nanda character (renamed Clara) passing unhappily through a series of enclosed worlds which are travesties of the convent's security: her own home, coloured by her scorn for her mother and her over-dependence on her father's approval; the country house of an aristocratic Catholic family, where the son and heir is accidentally killed while under her care; the tatty claustrophobic love-nest in Chelsea ('the Sugar House') where her first puerile marriage fails to be consummated; and the asylum, where she is taken by her father, after the violent exhilaration of a brief love affair with a young soldier has tipped her over into insanity. Up to her incarceration, Clara is increasingly possessed by lassitude, apathy, and 'an overall sense of guilt, not localised, as if . . . for some mysterious sin she did not remember having committed.' The legacy of her father's emotional demands and of the convent's training is a fear that her mental state may be a mortal sin: 'this sense that something in her had died and already exhaled a faint odour of corruption. A terrifying text slipped into her mind: "The lukewarm He shall spew out of His mouth." '

The fictions are to a large extent autobiographical. Like Jean Rhys, and like Colette (whose novels and stories she translated), Antonia White draws over and over again on the same key areas in her life: the convent, her madness, the asylum. She began writing *Frost in May* in 1915 after her expulsion from the Convent of the Sacred Heart at Roehampton, but before she took it up again in 1933 there had been a traumatic young-adulthood. Soon after her attempt to make a career as an actress, and her first marriage, she had a mental breakdown and was in Bethlem Asylum for ten months. When she came out in 1923 she went through the humiliating process of an annulment, married again, and lost her faith. She had a daughter by another man, her second marriage was annulled, and her father died feeling entirely disappointed in her. In 1930 she married Tom Hopkinson, by whom she had a second daughter. (All this was 'played out against a background of work' as a copy-editor and journalist.) During the 1930s there were frequent recurrences of what she referred to variously as 'neurasthenia', a 'mental smash', 'accidie', or 'the Beast'. She had four years of Freudian analysis ('a pretty rigorous mental discipline'), was divorced from Hopkinson in 1937, and returned to the Church in the early 1940s, a process recorded in the series of letters published in 1965 as *The Hound and the Falcon* (reissued in 1980 by Virago).

In these letters Antonia White refers ruefully to one of the side-effects of her mental history:

> I'm bad about writing and have a definite jam in my mind about it which *may* be permanent. I have a superb collection of beginnings . . . When you consider I wrote the first two chapters of *Frost in May* when I was 16 and the rest when I was over 30 you'll see how unresponsive and slow the machine is.

Her slow rate of creative work (as distinct from 'ephemeral journalism' of which she wrote 'about 150,000 [words] a year'), and her need repeatedly to recover certain crucial experiences, explains the range and nature of this volume of stories. Three of them date from before the completion of *Frost in May* in 1933. Of these, 'The House of Clouds' (1928) anticipates the

Bethlem section of *Beyond the Glass* (1954), which makes some additions, transpositions and changes (the 'house of clouds' becomes a 'house of mirrors') but which is extraordinarily close to the pre-analysis version of almost thirty years before. 'The Saint' (1928) introduces several of the characters and episodes of *Frost in May*, though it is written in the first and not the third person, and has a more comical, chatty tone than the novel. Only one story dates from the 'writer's block' period, a disturbing, callous little satire called 'The Exile' (1935). There are three stories from the 1940s. One, 'The Moment of Truth' (1941) returns her to a marriage which is breaking up because of the wife's mental illness and the husband's infidelity; one, 'The Rich Woman' (1943) anticipates the treatment of her first marriage in *The Sugar House* (1952). In the last story (not previously collected) the wheel comes full circle: 'The Surprise Visit' (1965) records a return to Bethlem, now the Imperial War Museum. Antonia White did make such a return visit in 1941, and mentions it lightly in her letters ('I've seen my old cell with a case of shells in it and a radiator which we lunatics would have greatly appreciated!'). But the need to recover the past stays with her. In the story, the woman who goes back succumbs to her memories of the place and collapses into insanity as though the fifteen intervening years have not been, though her intention was to undertake the visit 'coolly

iv

and unemotionally, at the right, the scientific moment.'

The pull between the controlling writer, digging up her past as though she were her own analyst, and the unredeemed, 'untreated' self in the fiction, unable to make coherent shape of, or distance herself from her state of mind, is characteristic. It's a strain which is both risky (the story may fail to get itself written at all) and fruitful, in that it informs the best of Antonia White's work: *Frost in May*, 'The Moment of Truth', 'The House of Clouds' and its matching section in *Beyond the Glass*. It reflects a temperamental quality: there is, she says, 'something in my nature which is touchy, harsh and, to many people, repellent. For myself that harsh streak is the only thing I value in myself and the thing that gives me any hope of some day doing some good work.' Analysis has strengthened that quality: 'The net result of this is that I do know a little about myself, as one might know a little about the engine of a car, and roughly what I can and cannot expect of the machine.' But it's also a noticeable attribute of one kind of woman's writing: the same shaping of dangerously unstable material is found in Virginia Woolf's treatment of Rachel's delirium in *The Voyage Out* (1915) and of Septimus's madness in *Mrs Dalloway* (1925), in Jean Rhys's rendering of a kind of self in *Wide Sargasso Sea* (1966), and in Charlotte Perkins Gilman's baroque monologue of

growing 'madness' in *The Yellow Wallpaper*
(1892).

All Antonia White's stories have a suscepti-
bility to material details which emerges in the
lighter pieces simply as sharp decoration: the
scum on the tea-cup and the 'white ring round
the iris' of Miss Hislop's eyes in 'The Exile'; the
smell of the nurse and the vulgar statuette on the
Cottage Hospital mantelpiece in 'Strangers';
Aunt Rose's mildewed clothes and the dusty
furnishings of her tiny flat in Vienna. In the more
disturbing stories details become alarming, un-
reliable. The husband's swinging dressing-gown
on the wall of the ship's cabin, or the sea-spider
brought to the dinner-table by the sinister Mme
Berrichon in 'The Moment of Truth' turn themselves into elements of a hostile universe. Flowers,
furnishings, clothes and ornaments all act as
parts of Belle Chandler's 'plot' against the
younger girl in 'The Rich Woman'. In 'The
House of Clouds', a remarkable and distressing
document, objects are dislocated, overbearing,
either as participants in Helen's delusions
('She could see birds flying across the sky, not
real birds, but bird-shaped kites, lined with
strips of white metal that flew on wire') or as
tools of an inexplicable persecution:

> The nurses caught and dragged her along a passage. The
> passage was like a long room; it had a shiny wooden floor
> with double iron tracks in it like the tracks of a model
> railway.

> A young man with a signet ring on his finger was bending over her, holding a funnel with a long tube attached. He forced the tube down her nose and began to pour some liquid down her throat.

In all the stories a twofold pain is felt. One aspect of this is the battle between an individual will and a stronger authority. As in *Frost in May*, the girl or woman pushes herself against what restricts her (the convent rules, the asylum's crude constraints, the husband's supervision, the 'rich woman's' coercion) to the point of self-destruction or self-abnegation. The other aspect is, as the volume's title indicates, a sense of strangeness. ' "Why look at me as if I were an enemy?" ' the husband says to Charlotte in 'The Moment of Truth'. ' "Not an enemy. A stranger," she said wearily.' That alienation between couples (also the subject of 'Strangers') is a symptom of a more profound estrangement between the self and the environment it must inhabit: hence the emphasis in Antonia White's work on institutions like hospitals and convents. ' "I can't inhabit the present any more" ', Charlotte says. It's a predicament enacted by the characters in the stories and by the writer of them, who must spring on herself a series of 'surprise visits' into her own past to see what she 'can and cannot expect of the machine'.

Hermione Lee, York 1980

Quotations are taken from the Virago editions of Antonia White's four novels and from *The Hound and the Falcon*, Virago 1980.

The Key

ANOTHER world,
 Its walls are thin,
But, oh, I cannot
 Enter in.

I feel its touch,
 I breathe its air,
How long before
 I enter there?

The key hangs close,
 My grasp is weak;
Oh, you who know,
 Take pity: speak.

The Moment of Truth

ON the stone floor inlaid with coats of arms, only a few couples were dancing, yet the hall was filled with the lisping of feet. The music was as insistent as the band striking up when a man falls from a trapeze.

'Hardly anyone is dancing,' said Charlotte to the unknown man beside her, 'yet whenever I put out my hand, I touch someone.' But the stranger seemed not to have heard her. All his attention was taken up with the piece of string which he was twisting into elaborate bends. At first she was hurt because he was ignoring her. Then she realized that he was telling her something by means of the string. She tried to read words in the loops and twists. He tied a slip-knot and drew the noose over one finger. 'Is that——?' she began, and checked herself. For she had made an absurd mistake. The man beside her was not a stranger, but her husband, Richard.

And was she after all at Faringay? There was something not quite right about the hall. Looking up, she read the motto on one of the dark arches, 'Ne crede Byron'. The arch: the gilt letters were just as she remembered them, but the words should have been 'Labor ipse Voluptas'.

2

She must keep quiet, ask no questions, draw attention to nothing, least of all to herself. Now the hall was entirely empty of dancers. But, though the band brayed like a steam organ, she could still hear the whispering feet. There was no longer anyone near her, but a woman laughed close by her ear and an invisible skirt brushed her knee.

With every second the danger was growing. Looking for a way of escape, Charlotte noticed a door she had never seen before. Printed on it in large Gothic letters was the word MURDER.

Now she knew that she could not be too careful. She must act very quietly, very normally. She walked over towards the buffet, feeling her way through the unseen dancers. They would not make room for her, but pressed against her, jostling and holding her back. She dared not wince or cry out, though she could feel hands passing up and down her spine, pinching her arms, stroking her throat. An invisible man embraced her, pushing his thighs against hers. A finger was thrust in her eye. A woman's bracelet caught in her hair. But, keeping back her terror, she went on slowly making her way through the crowd of laughing enemies.

By the buffet the space was clear. The man in the white cap carving a ham with a long, thin knife raised his head and looked at her with eyes

3

bolting from a doll's face. He leant over the table and ran the knife blade caressingly down her arm. 'I *know*,' he whispered. It had come. She must get out. In a second it would be too late.

'Richard! Richard! Richard!' she screamed from bursting lungs.

     .   .   .   .   .

The cry Charlotte heard as she broke through to the safer world was the thinnest wail, less audible than the pounding of her heart. She put out her hand to touch Richard, and her knuckles encountered only wood. She seemed to be lying in a coffin that heaved under her with a shuddering creak. Was she awake, or had she struggled out of one nightmare into another? She forced her eyes wide open and took deep gasps of breath. The air, smelling of oil and paint, was suffocating, but it was the air of the tangible world. Groping along the ledge, she found a switch and turned on the dim cabin light.

'Richard,' she said.

There was no answer.

Leaning over the edge of the bunk, she listened for his breathing. She heard nothing but the straining creak of the ship and the crash of the waves against the porthole. His dressing-gown swung towards her from the opposite wall and

4

stayed suspended at a wide angle till the wall swung forward to meet it. The wall itself swerved from the straight, and the dressing-gown lapsed back on to it. She stared at it as it swayed, hung suspended, and dropped until she began to feel its sickening rhythm behind her eyes and had to look away.

At last she made herself climb down and peer into the lower bunk. The sheets were folded with the precision of a hospital bed. On the pillow lay nothing but Richard's watch. She picked it up, looked at the time, and crouched back on the bunk, dangling the watch by its strap. It was half-past one; more than two hours since he had kissed her good-night and gone up on deck. Why had he left her for so long?

Ever since she had begun, a few months before, to have oppressive dreams, she counted on finding him near her when she fought out of them, always calling his name. He had learnt to slip an arm round her, even to mutter reassuring words, without waking from his sleep. Now that he was not there, when she needed him such bitterness rose up in her that she could feel an acrid taste in her mouth.

The next lurch of the narrow cabin flung his dressing-gown against her knee. Snatching it from the hook, she huddled into it, meaning to go up on deck and find him. But she felt sick. Her knees bent under her and she dropped back, stooping, on the bunk.

The cabin was growing smaller, hotter, more imprisoning every minute. She seemed to have swollen to enormous size. The heavy man's dressing-gown was stifling her, but she could not make the effort to take it off. Her skin pricked as if hairs were starting out of it. The bitterness vanished in the beginning of a terror worse than the nightmare, the waking terror from which there was no escape. She could neither bear to be alone in this dim, lurching cupboard nor get up strength to burst open the door. With eyes stiffening in their sockets, she could only crouch there, gripping the watch-strap as if it were a life-line.

Trying to keep the fear from closing in on her, she focused all her mind on the watch. To her it was part of Richard's body. The silver back was stained from four years' contact with his flesh. It had marked him too, printing its shape in a white fetter on his wrist. Night after night the beat of its tiny metal pulse had sounded like a second heart, a fraction of him that remained awake while he slept. It had become so intimately his that, fingering it in his absence, she seemed to be touching something to which she had no right.

6

She had not held it in her hand since she had taken it shining from its case and given it him the night before they were married. The next morning, just as she was leaving her room to go across to the church where his father was waiting to marry them, he had run into her, breathless and laughing.

'My watch, Charlotte! I can't be married without my watch! I've raced back from the altar for it.'

She remembered how he looked, bright-eyed and ruddy from the November wind, his hair sleeked, a flower in his coat—the picture of a bridegroom.

But, try as she would to hold the image, the tide of panic went on rising, sweeping her back from the real world. The watch slipped to the floor. She dropped back on the bunk with closed eyes and gasping mouth like a drowning woman beaten off from a lifeboat.

'Charlotte!'

His voice called her back. It sounded in the core of her ear, yet it seemed to come from another dimension, like the voice of the nurse to which one wakes after chloroform. She forced up her eyelids and looked at him. He filled the cabin, standing over her in his loose oilskin coat.

'Charlotte, dear, are you awake or asleep?'

7

With a huge effort she made herself open her mouth and speak, only to say in a dry whisper:

'Your watch. On the floor. Don't tread on it.'

He picked up the watch. His face, as it stooped to the level of hers, still glistened with spray, and his hair was damp and ruffled.

'What is the matter, Charlotte? Are you ill?'

'I had a bad dream,' she said, staring past him.

'And I wasn't there. I'm sorry.'

'What does it matter?'

'Oh, Charlotte, not that voice. And why look at me as if I were an enemy?'

'Not an enemy. A stranger,' she said wearily.

'I shouldn't have stayed away so long.'

There was regret in his tone, not the mechanical gentleness she had lately come to expect. It softened the shell of her hatred. She sat up and let him put his arm round her shoulder. Sitting side by side, their heads leaning together, their foreheads dropped, they seemed to be mourning a common loss.

'What was your dream, Charlotte?'

'I woke before it became too bad. It was about Faringay.'

'You are haunted by that house. Why do you keep dreaming about the past?'

'I can't inhabit the present any more.'

8

His arm tightened as the ship gave a lurch.

'We shouldn't be talking so late. We may be keeping people awake in the next cabin.'

She drew away from him in anger. Then she laughed.

'You inhabit the present all right.'

'It makes you so angry that I do. Yet one of us must.'

'Perhaps one is enough,' she said almost gaily.

He stood up and tried gently to draw her to her feet. But she shook her head and settled back on the bunk. He loomed above her, balancing on his strong legs, adjusting them to the movement of the ship.

'Don't you ever have dreams, Richard?'

'Mine don't make stories like yours.'

'Do you never have a dream that seems more true than life? That shows you something you never knew before—or were afraid to know?'

He began to wind his watch.

'Sometimes, perhaps.'

'You don't tell me them.'

She glanced up and saw his face set and heavy. In the dim light the shadows under his eyes were dark as bruises. She knew he was tired out, but she hardened to him.

'I don't always dream of the past, Richard.'

He went on turning the knob of his watch.

9

'You'll break the mainspring,' she cried in a burst of rage. Then, bitterly, 'I forgot. You'd never ill-treat a piece of *machinery*, would you?'

He laid the watch down carefully and took her by the wrist, pressing his fingers on it as if feeling her pulse.

'Charlotte!' he said quietly and urgently, 'Charlotte! You must get some sleep now.'

He pulled her up against the dead weight of her resistance.

'I'll help you into your bunk.'

'No. I feel sick.'

'You'll be better lying flat. It's beginning to calm down. Up on deck I could hardly keep my legs.'

'Then why did you stay so long?'

He kissed her forehead.

'Up you go. Carefully.'

As she scrambled up clumsily, a sudden roll shot her forehead against an iron staple, and Richard cried out.

'You needn't pity me about physical pain,' she said. 'It's a relief.'

'You don't want that heavy old dressing-gown. You'll be far too hot.'

She took it off and let it fall.

'I don't remember putting it on. I must be a little crazy.'

He smoothed her pillow, pulled the harsh sheets over her, and putting back her tangled hair, began to stroke her forehead. For a minute she lay with closed eyes, not resisting him. A tear oozed under her eyelid and crawled down her temple.

'Will you sleep now?' he said softly.

Her eyes sprang open.

'You say I always dream of the past. What about my other dream? The one about your leaving me?'

'You've dreamt that ever since we married, haven't you?' he said in his same soft voice, still stroking her head.

She jerked it away from his touch.

'I shall go on dreaming it. Until it comes true.'

'Has it ever been near coming true?'

'How should I know?' She closed her eyes once more. A wave exploded with a gentle crash against the porthole.

'If only we could open it and get some air,' said Richard.

Though Charlotte had withdrawn too far into herself to care about the heat or the reek of oil, she knew how they must sicken his wind-freshened senses. Yet she beat her fist against the ledge of the bunk, crying:

'You mean I am stifling you. Go on. Say it. Say it.'

'I will say nothing of the kind,' he whispered in patient fury.

She bared her teeth and tried to strike him, but he leaned over her, pinioning her shoulders like a lover or a murderer. She lay helpless for a moment, gasping with anger. Then suddenly she smiled.

'Why do I have to behave like this? Why can't you stop me?'

He smiled too and shook his head.

'Let me go now,' she said, speaking for the first time in her normal voice. 'You needn't hold me down. I am not dangerous.'

He took his hands from her shoulders and began to stroke her arm as if he were expertly and mechanically stroking an animal.

'I know,' he said.

She lay with closed eyes, quiet but unappeased. There was something she wanted to tell him, something urgent which kept flitting just out of reach of her thought like a forgotten name. He kissed her lightly and began, quietly as a thief, to lower himself into his own bunk. When she remembered what she had been groping for and softly called his name, he did not answer.

．　　．　　．　　．　　．

Their bedroom in the Hotel Berrichon was square and low-ceilinged, with a floor of red tiles arranged in a honeycomb pattern. Stiff yellow-lace curtains were looped back from the window that looked out over the whole expanse of the Baie de la Fresnaye. Madame Berrichon leered at Richard and Charlotte as she patted the red eiderdown of the enormous bed.

'You will hardly find a bed so comfortable in the whole of Brittany. My neighbours are satisfied with the old-fashioned *lits clos*—mere cupboards. But I am from Paris. I am civilized. I do not look on a bed as something in which one huddles oneself to sleep like an animal. In Paris we say that the bed is the battlefield of love.'

'Indeed,' said Richard, politely.

Charlotte turned away with a sigh of exasperation and began to pour water from the tiny cracked pitcher into the basin.

'Madame is annoyed?' said Madame Berrichon, in her hoarse, purring contralto. 'One does not say such things to English ladies? Forgive me. I am a person of impulses. I do not weigh my words.'

'Are we the only people staying here?' asked Richard.

'Yes, Monsieur. It is early in the season. And in any case few people care for a place so remote. Only those who wish to be alone with nature—or painters—or'—she lowered her heavy wrinkled lids—'lovers.'

'We only found it by accident,' Richard said, with an uneasy glance at Charlotte's back. 'We set out from St. Malo this morning, and we've been driving all day. My wife is very tired.'

'Believe me, it was no accident,' said Madame Berrichon. She faced him squarely, a solid, shapeless figure in her dark shawl and black calico skirt. A shaft from the setting sun struck her face like limelight, showing up the black down on her upper lip and the open pores of her yellow skin. 'Nothing happens by accident in this life. I had an intuition that you would come—so strong that I sent my husband into Matignon to buy *langoustes* and other good things. He will tell you my intuitions are always justified.'

'I am sure they are, Madame,' said Richard, meeting her eyes with a stare of polite impertinence.

'You laugh. You think I am a foolish old woman,' she said with dignity. 'It is true I do not concoct verses, only good dishes. But at heart, Monsieur, I am a poet. And whether you believe me or not, I am in touch with the most subtle forces of nature. I know by a certainty I cannot describe—a magnetic current in my blood perhaps—that you were both sent here for a purpose.

And if you do not know it, Madame your wife knows it, though she pretends not to listen to me.'

Charlotte did not speak or turn round until Madame Berrichon had glided out of the room, moving heavily yet swiftly over the tiles in her felt slippers.

'She's right. We can't get away even if we want to. She's a spider—a witch.'

'Well, she's got an ideal web or castle. It's an old sea-mill, she told me. Built right out into an arm of the bay. When the tide's up, there's water on three sides of the house.'

'In fact, we are really prisoners,' said Charlotte.

'You forget there's a fourth side. Stop thinking about Madame Berrichon and come and look out of the window.'

'I'm frightened of that old woman,' said Charlotte, moving slowly up to where Richard stood by the window.

'You should paint her and get her out of your system. You could do a wonderful portrait of her—a cross between a Balzac concierge and the Delphic sibyl.'

'I shall never paint again,' said Charlotte gloomily. 'I can't see outside things any more. Only beastly things in my own mind.'

He drew her arm through his with a brotherly gesture.

15

'All the same, come and look out of the window.'

They leant together on the low, narrow sill.

'You could dive straight out of the window into the sea,' she said.

'You'd better not try. See those dark patches under the surface? Rocks—jagged rocks too. You wouldn't have a chance.'

'What's happened to the sun? A few minutes ago there was a blazing sunset. Now look.'

The sky was overdrawn with fine cloud like a fog in the upper air. After the windless heat of the day, a breeze sprang up from nowhere, fanning gusts of invisible rain as fine as dust in their parched faces.

'Perhaps the wind and the rain come up with the tide,' said Richard. 'Can't you feel it's only on the surface? Underneath the air is still as hot and solid as ever. You can almost see the rain turning into steam.'

'How deep is the water?'

'Twenty or thirty feet I should say. Probably we're left high and dry when the tide goes out. Just rocks and mud.'

'What are those birds, Richard? The white ones. They're not ordinary gulls.'

Between the grey sky and the olive-green sea white birds skimmed to and fro, a few feet above

16

the surface, their black heads bent towards the water. Every now and then they dropped like stones into the sea, then flashed up again in an arrowy curve. Richard waited till one settled on an old boat moored to a ring in the wall.

'Look! do you see his forked tail? They're sea swallows: you can't see the fork when they fly—they move so fast—the feathers all whirl together.'

'Like spun glass: like the birds with spun-glass tails we had on the Christmas tree.'

For a moment Charlotte forgot everything in the pleasure of watching the shooting, diving swallows. Then she turned from the window with a sigh.

'I wish I were a bird. Or even a rock or a patch of seaweed. Anything—anything but a human being.'

She went to the basin and began to wash her hands. Richard threw himself on the bed.

'Is that water warm?'

'No. It's icy—like mountain water.'

He yawned. 'Then I can't shave. You'll have to put up with me with a beard.'

'You can't look worse than I do,' said Charlotte, peering at herself in a greenish-speckled mirror. Suddenly she turned and faced him.

'Richard, why didn't you tell me?'

17

'Tell you what?' he said, in a voice lazy, yet guarded.

'That I've suddenly aged ten years.'

'Don't talk nonsense.'

'You're not looking at me.'

'I don't have to. There's nothing the matter with your face. It's that absurd glass.'

'The glass can't give me those lines. Or those shadows under my eyes.'

'Then it's the way the light falls. Stop being morbid.'

Her face was strained and searching.

'Richard! seriously, I *do* look terrible, don't I?'

He smiled at the ceiling.

'Of course you look a little tired. Who wouldn't, after that night on the boat and driving all day in the sun and dust. Two nights' rest and you'll look wonderful.'

She turned her back on him again, fiercely dragging a comb through her soft, fair hair that had gone limp from the heat.

'I hate my face,' she muttered: 'hate it! hate it! hate it!'

'Well, I don't,' he said good-humouredly. He swung himself off the bed and stood up, stretching his firm, handsome, brown arms. 'Come down and have a drink. We both need one.'

The dining-room was large and dim, lit only by

18

three small windows on the landward side. It was paved with the same dull red honeycomb tiles as the bedroom and furnished only with two dark presses and a dozen tables covered with red-and-white oil-cloth. At the far end, like a huge-well-head filled with stones, the shaft which had once held the hoppers of the mill thrust up through the floor. Underneath, though muffled by the stones, the tide could be heard gurgling in the empty shaft.

They sat down at the only table that was laid. Through the window they could see a small, dusty courtyard with a battered table, a few iron chairs, and a fig-tree. A yellow mongrel was asleep on one of the chairs; at the table sat Monsieur Berrichon, a wizened little man in a beret and a faded blue blouse, sipping a glass of wine, round which the wasps hovered and buzzed.

Beside Charlotte's plate lay a passion-flower, a star of thick green-white petals with a fringe of blue rays. From the centre of the star four dark stamens stood up, lined with bright yellow pollen and three curious bosses like nail heads. She picked it up and sniffed its strong, fleshy scent.

'How did this come here? It couldn't be you, Richard?'

He smiled and shook his head.

Madame Berrichon's felt slippers shuffled on

the tiles behind her. Charlotte dropped the flower and turned to find the old woman at her elbow, holding out in both hands an enormous knobbed red sea-spider. The creature's body was larger than a crab; its long, spiky arms waved viciously and helplessly trying to clutch the black shawl.

'You see, Madame? I could not resist proving to you that we expected you. Tonight I can only give you a simple meal—but tomorrow, a little feast.'

Charlotte drew back from the waving, clutching tentacles.

'Aha! you are nervous? He is a wicked fellow, no? He would like to crush your hand with those pincers—but we are Christians, are we not? We repay evil with good. I have the water already boiling in my kitchen to give him a nice hot bath.'

'Please take it away,' said Charlotte, shuddering.

'Madame is too sensitive,' said Madame Berrichon, winking at Richard. 'I sympathize. I am sensitive myself—to a degree you would not understand. But one must be a realist too. Providence has arranged that many things should only be good and useful when they are dead.'

She retreated slowly to the kitchen, still talking half-threateningly, half-amorously to the sea-spider.

'Do you think it was she who put the passion-flower there?' asked Charlotte, when the kitchen door closed behind Madame Berrichon.

'She's quite capable of it.'

Charlotte pushed the flower away from her.

Louison, Madame's rosy-cheeked, eighteen-year-old niece, in her blue apron and sabots, trotted in with their soup. She glanced at the passion-flower and flushed.

'Madame is offended that I put this flower on the table?'

'Oh, was it you, Louison?' Charlotte drew it back to her. 'No, I love it. I was showing it to my husband.'

She felt herself blushing in her turn.

'But you see, Louison, I can't wear it, I haven't a pin.'

The girl took a pin from her apron and fastened the flower to Charlotte's dress. They both smiled.

'There, Madame. Now you look like a bride.'

Blushing again and glancing at Richard under her fingers, Louison picked up her tray and trotted off again, her sabots pattering like hooves on the tiles.

'There—you see,' said Richard triumphantly. 'It's not all black magic here.'

Charlotte fingered the flower, feeling suddenly old and exhausted.

'She's charming. All the same, it's a little ironical to be treated like a bride.'

As she drooped, Richard seemed to revive. His eyes widened and shone as he filled their glasses with the cheap red wine.

'Drink up,' he said, looking aggressively young and healthy. 'Here's to your getting better.'

Charlotte drank too.

'A thoroughly sensible, practical wish. If Louison heard it, that would be the end of her honeymoon illusions.'

'Charlotte, you know as well as I do that nothing can go right for us till you're cured.'

'Cured of what? There's nothing the matter with me.'

'I wish that were true.'

'Then act as if it were,' she said recklessly. 'You treat me as if I were sick or mad, and I become sick and mad. It's your fault.'

He opened his mouth as if he were going to speak. Instead, he finished his glass and filled it up again.

'Perhaps the only thing that's really wrong with us, Charlotte, is that we don't drink enough.'

'Maybe it's as simple as that. You always used to say you hated drink.'

'I've said a lot of idiotic things.'

Charlotte stared at him. His face, which she was accustomed to seeing gentle, controlled, almost too anxious to please, looked defiant, even a little dissolute.

'Richard, you're different in some way.'

'Well, shouldn't one be different on a holiday? Or perhaps you haven't seen me for so long you've forgotten what I'm like?'

'Nearly six weeks. We've never been apart so long before.'

'No.'

'It's supposed to be a good thing for people who are married, isn't it?'

For no reason—or perhaps because of the wine —she suddenly began to feel confident, almost exultant.

'I'm sure it's an *excellent* thing,' she said emphatically.

'Is it?' He sipped his drink, frowning.

'I've been such a *fool*, Richard.' She took a deep gulp of the harsh wine. 'Working myself up into such a state over nothing. But I can be different, too, you'll see.'

'You couldn't help being ill.'

It was again the voice she dreaded; gentle, reasonable, placating. But she could ignore it.

'I'm not ill, I tell you. I've just been giving way

23

to myself. Illusion, nothing but illusion. But everything's going to be all right now. Don't I look different already?'

She smiled theatrically, feeling the flesh stretched and tingling over her cheekbones.

'You look splendid. All the same, you must take things quietly for a bit.'

She made a face.

'You're worse than the doctors.'

'You always rush things so. I get giddy trying to keep up with you.'

'I'd like to get the car out and drive for miles. Let's get away from the old witch and her mill.'

'Wait until tomorrow. You don't know how tired you are.'

She put down her glass and sighed.

'It's no good. I believe you want to depress me. You want me to be wretched. So that everyone can pity you and say what a wonderful husband you are to that tiresome woman.'

'Don't talk nonsense,' he said, gently.

'We're never in the same mood at the same moment. Why is it? A moment ago, you were gay and I felt flat. Now I'm gay, and you're wilting before my eyes; is it the same with all married people?'

'I don't know: I daresay.' He lit a cigarette. 'Is there anything you'd like to do?'

She smoked for a minute or two, greedily and mechanically, scattering ash on the oilcloth.

'No, nothing. You make me feel there's no point in doing anything.'

'I'm not much good to you, am I, Charlotte?'

He swept up the ash she had dropped into a neat little heap.

'You're too good, that's just the trouble. Too patient, too considerate. Everything I do irritates you; even the way I smoke a cigarette.'

'Oh, I can put up with that,' he laughed. 'My tidiness is a vice; something you have to put up with.'

'If you only had one grain of viciousness or disorderliness.'

He blew the little heap of ashes on to the floor.

'You know me through and through, don't you? No wonder you find me so dull.'

'I don't know you,' she said thoughtfully. 'I only know what you say and do.'

'Isn't that enough? The trouble is I'm too simple for you.'

'You're not simple: you're not simple at all,' she sighed. 'Or am I the only woman incapable of understanding you?'

'You've such an itch for understanding things, haven't you? Why can't you accept me as I am?'

25

'I do more than accept you,' she said quietly, 'I love you.'

He looked down, avoiding her eyes, his face heavy and clouded.

'Yes. I suppose you feel that is more.'

Her throat went dry.

'You don't want me to love you. Is that it? Does that mean——?'

He would not let her finish. 'Don't let's discuss what words mean. I tell you we won't get anywhere with words.'

'Why not, with the right words?' she insisted obstinately.

He jerked his head like a horse on a too-short rein.

'I tell you, I haven't your idolatrous respect for words.'

'Yet you're so careful with them. You never exaggerate as I do. Never say more than you mean.'

He smiled. She noticed again how tight-lipped and secret his mouth was in contrast to the almost aggressive frankness of the eyes. The lips always looked bruised and chafed as if they were made of older, more worn material than the fresh skin of his face.

'I expect it's just part of the tidiness that infuriates you so.'

'At any rate you're honest. I cling to that.'

'Poor Charlotte. It's a negative thing to cling to.'

'It's enough,' she boasted, knowing that she lied.

. . . . .

Charlotte lay back in the great bed watching Richard moving about the room, unpacking her suitcase, and folding her clothes.

'Why don't you let me do anything for myself tonight?' she said.

'You're tired.'

'But it could all wait till tomorrow.'

He smiled and went on inexorably arranging everything in perfect order. When everything was in place, he spread his heavy dressing-gown over her feet.

'You'll be cold in that great icy bed.'

'But aren't you coming to bed yourself?'

'Very soon. I'm going to take a turn outside first.'

Her face stiffened with disappointment as she watched him slipping a jacket over his short-sleeved shirt.

'Just as you like,' she said listlessly.

'Don't be angry, Charlotte. You know what a fool I am about strange places. I can't settle down till I've got my bearings.'

She managed to smile.

'Then of course you must go.'

'You can be an angel when you want to.'

She laughed, pleased at having controlled herself.

'You're thinking, why can't I always be?'

'Yes, why can't you?' he mocked.

'I'll tell you,' she said, sliding her fingers under the cuff of his jacket and stroking his bare wrist. 'It wears one down, being married to a man who always gives such excellent reasons for everything he does.'

He kissed her hand, disengaged himself gently, and went out, closing the door stealthily as if she were already asleep.

But she was no longer sleepy. Fighting down an impulse to call him back, she sat up in bed, clenching her hands round her knees and staring in front of her. Because it was not yet quite dark outside, she felt like a child sent to bed for punishment. She got up and padded round the room; the cold, slippery tiles were ice to her bare feet. The mantelpiece distracted her for a few minutes with its load of photographs, oleographs of the Sacred Heart and the Little Flower, black-framed memorial cards, and brass vases filled with immortelles, all set out with precision like the ornaments of an altar on a starched cloth edged

with crochet lace. She examined the photographs
with interest, recognizing Madame in a wedding-
group, Louison in the long white dress and veil of
a First Communicant, Monsieur Berrichon,
twenty years younger, in an ill-fitting army uniform. But these were quickly exhausted. How
was she to kill time till Richard came back? She
could not lie in the cold bed staring and thinking.
In the last months she had become afraid to think.
Her very thoughts were tarnished. They split and
unravelled into meaningless ends. Often she believed she was going insane. Something inside
her seemed to have died and to be filling her mind,
even her body, with corruption. Now it was as if
she had accidentally overheard a terrible secret
and that everything she did or thought was an attempt to stop her ears and forget. At other times
she was like a person who must guess an impossible riddle on pain of death and who has only a
few hours left in which to find the answer. Out-
wardly her life went on as before, except that for
some months she had been growing languid, irrit-
able, and prone to dreams which oppressed her
for days.

She had come away for this holiday determined
to shake off the shadow. With all his vigorous
sanity, Richard himself had lately begun to look
moody and careworn. She guessed it was for his

sake as much as hers that he had made her give up
work for a time and go away alone to the country.
It had been dull misery being away from him, yet
now that she saw him again she felt more shut
away than ever, as a drowning man feels his isola-
tion more bitterly when he can see people walking
on the shore. There were moments when she
hated him, but they were nothing to the loathing
she felt for herself. Yet even her self-hatred was
not pure; it had an element of gloating in it; a
strain of vile pleasure, as well as disgust.

Tonight, she told herself, she would not give
way to it. Already she could feel herself slipping.
When Richard came back there must not be a re-
petition of the night on the boat. What could she
do to pass the time in a sane, normal way until she
felt safe enough to put out the light? She remembered that there was a detective story in the
pocket of the coat Richard had worn on the journey. She opened the door of the cupboard and
saw the coat hanging inside. The green-and-
white cover of the book showed over the top of
the pocket. As she pulled it out a letter fell out
with it. It was a thick letter in a blue envelope,
unopened. She picked it up and stared at it, for
she knew the writing. Her immediate thought
was, 'This is really meant for me.' The conviction was so strong that she was on the point of

opening it, though it was clearly addressed to 'Richard Crane'. She glared again at the envelope, as if by doing so she could change what was written on it. Then she saw it was not addressed to their London house, but to a poste restante near Waterloo. The shock was so great that she felt nothing but a mild exhilaration. The exhilaration had nothing to do with her mind, which remained perfectly blank; it was altogether physical, as if she had drunk something warm and stimulating.

There was a knock at the door. Thinking it was Richard, she slipped the letter into the coat pocket and darted back into bed, pulling the sheets up to her chin. She could feel that her eyes were shining, and her face set in a mask of bright expectancy as she called out, 'Come in.'

It was Madame Berrichon, carrying a steaming glass on a saucer with the air of a priestess carrying a sacred vessel.

'I had a little conversation with Monsieur, your husband,' she said, as she majestically approached the bed. 'It appears you have been indisposed, Madame, and have bad nights. I have taken the liberty of bringing you something to make you sleep.'

A thought flashed up in Charlotte's mind; a thought so fantastic that she did not attempt to brush it away. 'He has sent this woman to poison me.'

Out loud she said politely, 'It is kind of you, Madame, but drugs don't have the effect on me. I sleep better without them.'

'This is no drug, Madame. I myself abominate drugs. It is a tisane made of wholesome natural substances, a distillation of passion-flowers, to be exact.'

She glanced at the passion-flower, wilting in a glass on the chest of drawers.

'A charming flower, no? Alive it gives us pleasure; dead it gives us peace.'

'My husband made a mistake, Madame Berrichon. There is nothing the matter with me.'

Madame Berrichon stooped and brought her face close to Charlotte's, fixing her with huge eyes the colour of black coffee.

'I do not need to be told you are ill,' she said, in her hoarse purr. 'I do not judge as doctors. I judge from deeper sources. And I tell you are not only ill, but in grave danger.'

'Nonsense,' said Charlotte, wishing she could laugh, yet feeling her throat contract. 'You are trying to frighten me. Why?'

'Certainly not, Madame. I am speaking only for your good. How do I know? Because Providence has given me a nature of extraordinary sensibility. And I pay a price for it. When others suffer, I suffer in every fibre of my being. To-night you will sleep, but I, I shall not close my eyes.'

'You are too sensitive, Madame,' said Charlotte coldly, remembering the sea-spider.

'Sensitive, Madame, that is too banal a word. Good Catholic as I am, I dare not go to Mass. The chanting disturbs my nerves too much.' She turned up her eyes till only half the iris showed in the blood-shot, yellowish whites. 'Believe me, Madame, I have only to see my Piboulette with her ducklings, to think of my dog Nanasse, to weep like a child.'

Madame Berrichon brought her eyes into focus again and thrust the glass into Charlotte's limp hand.

'You must drink, Madame. Before it gets cold.'

Powerless, only wanting to be rid of the woman, Charlotte took a sip of a hot liquid, bitter as alum.

Madame Berrichon watched her greedily, anchoring her hands to her solid hips.

'A trifle bitter? There are many bitter things in life as you, Madame, are still too young to know. But this bitterness brings sweetness. When you have drained every drop—piff, paff—you will be

33

in the arms of Morpheus. So deeply asleep that your charming husband on his return might suppose you dead. So, another little, little sip.'

On a sudden impulsion Charlotte launched the glass through the open window. It fell with a faint splash into the sea.

'Softly, Madame,' said the woman without moving. She gave an imperturbable, pitying leer. 'You see, I am not angry. With hysterics, one must be patient.'

'I am not an hysteric,' Charlotte muttered between her teeth.

'Quite so, quite so, my poor little lady,' the other purred. 'What more natural? So handsome a husband—of course one would not wish him to find one asleep. So very sound asleep too.'

Charlotte felt locked as if in one of her nightmares. She bit her lips so as not to scream for Richard. She looked wildly round the room, staring imploringly at each object he had so carefully arranged, his brushes, a jar of brilliantine, her own powder bowl, as if they could exorcize this presence. But implacably her eyes were drawn back to Madame Berrichon's face.

'He is late, is he not, the charming husband?' said Madame Berrichon, moving away very slowly but still fixing her with the obscene eyes of a witch and a midwife.

34

She did not speak again until she reached the door.

'Believe me, Madame, I do not hold your ingratitude against you. You are not responsible for your actions. I have done what I could. You prefer to reject it. I hope you will not suffer for it.'

She lingered a moment in the open door, like an actress leaving the stage.

'I too, Madame, have a good husband.'

Then, shrugging her black woollen shoulders, she added very softly with a cunning, confederate smile:

'All the same, my little lady, when I look for warmth, for understanding, for fidelity, I turn, not to any human being, but to Nanasse my dog.'

. . . . . .

When Richard came back an hour later, he found Charlotte sitting bolt upright in bed, her hands knotted round her raised knees. She did not turn her head as he came in, but glared straight in front of her with round, glassy eyes. A bright-blue woollen scarf sagging round her shoulders took all the colour from her face. She looked at once like a sick child and an immeasurably old woman.

'Charlotte,' he said, feeling his heart contract with pity and terror. She did not speak or move. He took a step towards her.

35

'My dear, what is it? Are you ill? Have you had a dream?'

Still not looking at him, she spoke at last in a small, dry, high-pitched voice.

'Curious, aren't you? For such a *very* incurious chap.'

The pert words coming out of the stiff, livid face shocked him as if a corpse had begun to giggle. He sat down on the bed, and taking her by both shoulders began to shake her.

'Charlotte, for God's sake.'

Her body rocked to and fro under his hands like a doll's. When he left off shaking her she went on in exactly the same tone.

'You might at least be decently polite to her. After all, she is a friend of mine.'

Though he was in the direct line of her stare, he felt she could not see him.

'Charlotte,' he said quietly. 'Can you hear me speaking?'

Her expression changed. She turned her head as if she expected to find him at her side.

'Yes,' she answered fretfully. 'Of course I can hear you. What are you saying?'

Still quietly, he went on:

'Now will you turn your head and look at *me*.'

There was a long pause before her head very slowly came round.

36

'And now, Charlotte, will you tell me what and whom you are talking about?'

Her fine, almost invisible eyebrows went up. The eyes grew rounder still.

'Oh, *that*,' she said, like an impudent child. 'Didn't you know?'

'For Heaven's sake, stop this.'

He crouched forward, staring back at her like a hypnotist. Her eyes stayed blank and glassy; then a flicker of helpless terror came and went like the dart of a fin under ice.

'My dear, you *must* tell me. What is it I've done? Or that you imagine I've done?'

At last her eyelids relaxed. She tried to speak and could not, until she had passed her tongue two or three times over her dry lips.

'How do I know? I don't read letters.' She closed her eyes and added in a whisper, 'Yet.'

He let out the breath he had been holding on a long sigh.

Sitting back on the bed, he took her hands in his. She struggled for a moment to tug them away, then let them lie cold and inert in his grip.

'Listen to me,' he said, 'You are torturing yourself in your imagination. About what?'

'You should know.' Her voice was reasonable but aloof.

'I will tell you what I think. You have found a

letter written to me by'—he swallowed—'by someone we both know.'

'By Rachel Summerhill,' she said loudly.

'Mightn't there be a dozen explanations of that besides the one you're thinking of?'

'Even you can't invent a dozen reasons on the spur of the moment,' she said, glib as an actress.

He let go of her hands abruptly.

'All right, if you want a scene, we'll have a scene. God knows I ought to be good at them by now.' He stood up.

She clutched wildly at him.

'No Richard, no Richard': her face crumpled up. 'I'll behave myself. Only don't be angry, don't leave me alone.'

'I'm not going.'

She put her hands on her cheeks as if to hold the skin and muscles in place.

'It's the not knowing I can't stand. I don't care how bad it is. You must tell me.'

'Suppose there's nothing to tell?'

She examined him with an old, searching, impersonal gaze. He gazed back at her unflinchingly.

'Your eyes never tell anything.'

'I'll answer any question you like.'

'Truthfully?'

'Yes. But, Charlotte, for both our sakes, think carefully before you ask.'

Suddenly she sighed, looking at him almost with friendliness.

'I wish I had no memory.'

'So do I.' He risked a faint smile.

She looked not at his face, but at the coat pocket over his heart.

'Rachel Summerhill. Somehow I didn't think she'd be the first. If she is the first.' She was silent for a minute. Then she began to mutter, like a child muttering to itself but meaning to be overheard. 'It doesn't make sense. I used to have to force him to stay in the days she came to see us. He said she was such a bore. What was it he called her? An American college virgin carrying the torch of knowledge on graduation day.'

He put his hand under her chin and lifted her head, gripping her jaw so firmly that she winced.

'Ask your questions. Or keep quiet,' he said roughly.

She wrenched her face away.

'Was it pleasant, making love with her? Who enjoyed it most, you or Rachel?'

In spite of himself, his hands flew up towards her neck. She gave a spurt of excited laughter.

'You don't have to answer now.'

But the words he was trying to keep back burst

out, not through his throat, it seemed to him, but through his ribs. Automatically he put both hands on his chest as if to stop a flow of blood as he heard himself say:

'It was the only real thing that ever happened to either of us.'

Even then, Charlotte was so silent, that for a whole minute, he could believe he had not spoken and was merely watching words, written in smoke, fading on the air. He believed it until he looked at Charlotte's face and saw on it the same fear and exaltation he could feel on his own. For what seemed a long time they confronted each other, each searching the other's face like a mirror, in an intimacy of disaster.

A gust of wind blew out the stiff lace curtains at the window. Charlotte gave a long, shuddering sigh like a person waking from an anæsthetic. Her calmed face suddenly decomposed. She flung herself on Richard, tearing at his coat, butting his chest with her head.

He did not resist, but let her hammer him with blind, childish blows. Her whole body shook with dry sobs of anger. Finally, weak and breathless, she stopped battering at him and tried to push him away. He remained immovable, secure in himself and strong enough to pity her.

Charlotte dropped back, exhausted, on the pillows. Then, staring at the ceiling, she began a long, monotonous babble like the babble in delirium. At first he tried not to listen. Then in spite of himself he was sucked into these endless coils of words. She raved quietly on and on, not attacking him, but coldly, ferociously accusing herself. For long intervals she would show no consciousness of his being there, then she would implore him to go farther away.

'It's not safe for anyone to come near me. You don't understand. I am poisoned, poisoned right through.'

He did not dare to deny or to interrupt. The terrible words multiplied and multiplied, till he seemed to be watching the multiplication, cell by cell, of a cancer. He clenched his hands till the nails were white. He longed, like a fish gasping for water, not for Rachel herself, but for the thought of Rachel; cool, limited, single. But the thought of her could no more form in his mind than a snowflake could form in a hot room. It seemed to him that, for all eternity, he would never see anything but the lace curtains, the naked electric light, the photographs, the harsh blue scarf and Charlotte's distorted face. To shut them out, he hid his face in his hands. But he could not shut out the voice. It went on: a rise and fall of sound in which he no longer distinguished words.

Then abruptly, it stopped. Other different noises followed. They conveyed nothing to him. He did not look up. He could feel Charlotte was no longer there in the bed. But he could not look up. A long time seemed to pass. Then a rasping, metallic noise behind him made him start so violently that he thought he must have fallen asleep. Uncovering his face and jumping up, he saw Charlotte at the wide-open window, carefully hoisting herself on to the ledge outside. In two steps he was behind her, holding her round the waist. She crouched down on the ledge and turned a blind, set face to him, not struggling, but resigning herself to his hold. They stood for a moment in a grotesque embrace; then, with the force of an uncoiling spring, Charlotte threw herself forward, nearly dragging him with her. Lurching half over the sill, he could see far below the dark masses of slippery, jagged rock, half-bared by the ebbing tide. He regained his balance and braced his knees, making his thighs and legs heavy. She was struggling now with unbelievable fury like a sail full of wind. His arms turned numb; his feet slithered on the floor, but he still did not let go. Suddenly Charlotte seemed to dwindle to half her size. Turning, she slipped through his arms like a fish, and dropped down over the sill. For a second her white face hung suspended in the frame of the open window, then disappeared, leaving only the two clinging hands. Richard reeled back, too weak to make any more effort.

The hands were relaxing their grip. They no longer seemed to have any connexion with Charlotte. He found himself watching them impersonally, waiting for them to disappear. His head was beginning to clear. He drew a deep breath of the cold, sea air and felt deeply refreshed. Now his head was perfectly clear. It contained a single thought.

'I want her to die,' he said to himself.

In the overwhelming relief of acknowledging it, his muscles suddenly asserted themselves and adjusted themselves with extraordinary skill. He made a dive forward from his hips, reached down, caught Charlotte under the armpits and dragged her up through the window. A tremendous wave of exultation in his own strength, in the exquisitely stressed and balanced movement he had just made, went over him. The limp dead weight of her body as he pulled her in and held her against him, her feet dangling, seemed no more than the weight of a small animal. He lowered her gently till her feet touched the floor. She leant on him unresisting, her head against his shoulder.

Still with one arm round her, he closed the window and pulled the curtains. Then he lifted her up, laid her on the bed, turned out the light, and lay down beside her. She was still panting and shivering. He pulled his thick dressing-gown over them both and waited till her breathing was calm before he spoke. He was no longer frightened of anything he might say to her.

'Silly Charlotte. Why did you have to do that?'

She lay against him with an abandonment of trust he had never before felt in her.

'You wanted me dead,' she said peacefully.

He started, but she neither stiffened nor shrank away.

'You said so. Didn't you know?' Her voice was only a sleepy murmur.

He was too drunk with delicious torpor to answer. There was no more need for words; for the first time in their life together they were in complete accord. As they sank into the same profound sleep, they did not press closer, but their breathing gradually timed itself to the same rhythm till, at the vanishing point of consciousness, a single pulse seemed to beat through their two bodies.

The House of Clouds

THE night before, Helen had tried to drown
herself. She did not know why, for she had
been perfectly happy. The four of them,
she and Robert and Dorothy and Louis, had been
getting supper. Louis had been carrying on one
of his interminable religious arguments, and she
remembered trying to explain to him the differ-
ence between the Virgin Birth and the Immaculate Conception as she carried plates out of the
kitchen. And then, suddenly, she had felt extraordinarily tired and had gone out into the little
damp courtyard and out through the gate into the
passage that led to the Thames. She wasn't very
clear what happened next. She remembered that
Robert had carried her back to Dorothy's room
and had laid her on the bed and knelt beside her
for a long time while neither of them spoke. And
then they had gone back into the comfortable
noise and warmth of Louis's studio next door, and
the others had gone on getting supper exactly as
if nothing had happened. Helen had sat by the
fire, feeling a little sleepy and remote, but amaz-
ingly happy. She had not wanted any supper,
only a little bread and salt. She was insistent
about the salt, because salt keeps away evil spirits,

45

and they had given it to her quietly without any fuss. They were gentle with her, almost reverent. She felt they understood that something wonderful was going to happen to her. She would let no one touch her, not Robert even. It was as if she were being charged with some force, fiery and beautiful, but so dangerous that a touch would explode it.

She did not remember how she got home. But today had been quite normal, till at dinner-time this strong impulse had come over her that she must go to Dorothy's, and here, after walking for miles in the fog, she was. She was lying in Dorothy's bed. There was a fire in the room, but it could not warm her. She kept getting up and wandering over to the door and looking out into the foggy courtyard. Over and over again, gently and patiently, as if she were a child, Dorothy had put her back to bed again. But she could not sleep. Sometimes she was in sharp pain; sometimes she was happy. She could hear herself singing over and over again, like an incantation:

O Deus, ego amo te
Nec amo te ut salves me
Nec quia non amantes te
Aeterno punis igne.

The priest who had married her appeared by her bed. She thought he was his own ghost come to give her the last sacraments and that he had died at that very moment in India. He twisted his rosary round her wrist. A doctor came too; the Irish doctor she hated. He tried to give her an injection, but she fought him wildly. She had promised someone (was it Robert?) that she would not let them give her drugs. Drugs would spoil the sharpness of this amazing experience that was just going to break into flower. But, in spite of her fighting, she felt the prick of the needle in her arm, and sobbing and struggling still, she felt the thick wave of the drug go over her. Was it morphia? Morphia, a word she loved to say, lengthening the first syllable that sounded like the note of a horn. 'Morphia, mo-orphia, put an "M" on my forehead,' she moaned in a man's voice.

Morning came. She felt sick and mortally tired. The doctor was there still; her father, in a brown habit, like a monk, sat talking to him. Her father came over to the bed to kiss her, but a real physical dislike of him choked her, and she pushed him away. She knew, without hearing, what he and the doctor had been talking about. They were going to take her away to use her as an experiment. Something about the war. She was willing to go; but when they lifted her out of bed she cried desperately, over and over again, for Robert.

47

She was in a cab, with her head on a nurse's shoulder. Her father and two other men were there. It seemed odd to be driving through South Kensington streets in broad daylight, dressed only in one of Dorothy's nightgowns and an old army overcoat of Robert's. They came to a tall house. Someone, Louis, perhaps, carried her up flights and flights of steps. Now she was in a perfectly ordinary bedroom. An old nurse with a face she liked sat by the fire; a young one, very pink and white and self-conscious, stood near her. Helen wandered over to the window and looked out. There went a red bus, normal and reassuring. Suddenly the young nurse was at her elbow, leading her away from the window.

'I shouldn't look out of the window if I were you, dear,' she said in a soft hateful voice. 'It's so ugly.' Helen let herself be led away. She was puzzled and frightened; she wanted to explain something; but she was tired and muddled; she could not speak. Presently she was in bed, alone but for the old nurse. The rosary was still on her wrist. She felt that her parents were downstairs, praying for her. Her throat was dry; a fearful weariness weighed her down. She was in her last agony. She must pray. As if the old nurse understood, she began the 'Our Father' and 'Hail Mary'. Helen answered. Decade after decade

48

they recited in a mechanical rhythm. There were cold beads on Helen's forehead, and all her limbs felt bruised. Her strength was going out of her in holy words. She was fighting the overpowering sleepiness that she knew was death. 'Holy Mary, Mother of God,' she forced out in beat after beat of sheer will-power. She lapsed at last. She was dead, but unable to leave the flesh. She waited, light, happy, disembodied.

Now she was a small child again and the nurse was the old Nanny at the house in Worcestershire. She lay very peacefully watching the nurse at her knitting under the green lamp. Pleasant thoughts went through her head of the red-walled kitchen garden, of the frost on the rosemary tufts, of the firelight dancing in the wintry panes before the curtains were drawn. Life would begin again here, a new life perfected day by day through a new childhood, safe and warm and orderly as this old house that smelt of pines and bees-wax. But the nightmares soon began. She was alone in a crypt watching by the coffin of a dead girl, an idiot who had died at school and who lay in a glass-topped coffin in her First Communion dress, with a gilt paper crown on her head. Helen woke up and screamed.

Another nurse was sitting by the green lamp.

'You must be quiet, dear,' said the nurse.

There were whispers and footsteps outside.

'I hear she is wonderful,' said a woman's voice.

'Yes,' said another, 'but all the conditions must be right, or it will be dangerous for her.'

'How?'

'You must all dress as nurses,' said the second voice, 'then she thinks she is in a hospital. She lives through it again, or rather, they do.'

'Who . . . the sons?'

'Yes. The House of Clouds is full of them.'

One by one, women wearing nurses' veils and aprons tiptoed in and sat beside her bed. She knew quite well that they were not nurses; she even recognized faces she had seen in picture papers. These were rich women whose sons had been killed, years ago, in the war. And each time a woman came in, Helen went through a new agony. She became the dead boy. She spoke with his voice. She felt the pain of amputated limbs, of blinded eyes. She coughed up blood from lungs torn to rags by shrapnel. Over and over again, in trenches, in field hospitals, in German camps, she died a lingering death. Between the bouts of torture, the mothers, in their nurses' veils, would kiss her hands and sob out their gratitude.

'She must never speak of the House of Clouds,' one said to another.

And the other answered:

'She will forget when she wakes up. She is going to marry a soldier.'

Months, perhaps years, later, she woke up in a
small, bare cell. The walls were whitewashed and
dirty and she was lying on a mattress on the floor,
without sheets, with only rough, red-striped
blankets over her. She was wearing a linen
gown, like an old-fashioned nightshirt, and she
was bitterly cold. In front of her was the blank
yellow face of a heavy door without a handle of
of any kind. Going over to the door, she tried
frantically to push it open. It was locked. She began to call out in panic and to beat on the door till
her hands were red and swollen. She had forgotten her name. She did not know whether she
were very young or very old; a man or a woman.
Had she died that night in Dorothy's studio?
She could remember Dorothy and Robert, yet
she knew that her memory of them was not quite
right. Was this place a prison? If only, only her
name would come back to her.

Suddenly the door opened. A young nurse was
there, a nurse with a new face. As suddenly as the
door had opened, Helen's own identity flashed up
again. She called wildly, 'I know who I am. I'm
Helen Ryder. You must ring up my father and
tell him I'm here. I must have lost my memory.
The number is Western 2159.'

The nurse did not answer, but she began to laugh. Slowly, mockingly, inch by inch, though Helen tried with all her strength to keep it open, she closed the door.

The darkness and the nightmare came back. She lost herself again; this time completely. For years she was not even a human being; she was a horse. Ridden almost to death, beaten till she fell, she lay at last on the straw in her stable and waited for death. They buried her as she lay on her side, with outstretched head and legs. A child came and sowed turquoises round the outline of her body in the ground, and she rose up again as a horse of magic with a golden mane, and galloped across the sky. Again she woke on the mattress in her cell. She looked and saw that she had human hands and feet again, but she knew that she was still a horse. Nurses came and dragged her, one on each side, to an enormous room filled with baths. They dipped her into bath after bath of boiling water. Each bath was smaller than the last, with gold taps that came off in her hands when she tried to clutch them. There was something slightly wrong about everything in this strange bathroom. All the mugs were chipped. The chairs had only three legs. There were plates lying about with letters round the brim, but the letters never read the same twice running. The nurses looked like human beings, but Helen knew quite well that they were wax dolls stuffed with hay.

They could torture her for all that. After the hot baths, they ducked her, spluttering and choking, into an ice-cold one. A nurse took a bucket of cold water and splashed it over her, drenching her hair and half-blinding her. She screamed, and nurses, dozens of them, crowded round the bath to laugh at her. 'Oh, Nelly, you naughty, naughty girl,' they giggled. They took her out and dried her and rubbed something on her eyes and nostrils that stung like fire. She had human limbs, but she was not human; she was a horse or a stag being prepared for the hunt. On the wall was a looking-glass, dim with steam.

'Look, Nelly, look who's there,' said the nurses.

She looked and saw a face in the glass, the face of a fairy horse or stag, sometimes with antlers, sometimes with a wild, golden mane, but always with the same dark, stony eyes and nostrils red as blood. She threw up her head and neighed and made a dash for the door. The nurses caught and dragged her along a passage. The passage was like a long room; it had a shiny wooden floor with double iron tracks in it like the tracks of a model railway. The nurses held her painfully by the armpits so that her feet only brushed the floor. The passage was like a musty old museum. There were wax flowers under cases and engravings of Queen Victoria and Balmoral. Suddenly the nurses opened a door in the wall, and there was her cell again. They threw her down on the mattress and went out, locking the door.

She went to sleep. She had a long nightmare about a girl who was lost in the dungeons under an old house on her wedding-day. Just as she was, in her white dress and wreath and veil, she fell into a trance and slept for thirty years. She woke up, thinking she had slept only a few hours, and found her way back to the house, and remembering her wedding, hurried to the chapel. There were lights and flowers and a young man standing at the altar. But as she walked up the aisle, people pushed her back, and she saw another bride going up before her. Up in her own room, she looked in the glass to see an old woman in a dirty satin dress with a dusty wreath on her head. And somehow, Helen herself was the girl who had slept thirty years, and they had shut her up here in the cell without a looking-glass so that she should not know how old she had grown.

And then again she was Robert, endlessly climbing up the steps of a dark tower by the sea, knowing that she herself was imprisoned at the top. She came out of this dream suddenly to find herself being tortured as a human being. She was lying on her back with two nurses holding her down. A young man with a signet ring on his finger was bending over her, holding a funnel with a long tube attached. He forced the tube down her nose and began to pour some liquid down her throat. There was a searing pain at the back of her nose: she choked and struggled, but they held her down ruthlessly. At last the man drew out the tube and dropped it coiling in a basin. The nurses released her, and all three went out and shut the door.

This horror came at intervals for days. She grew to dread the opening of the door, which was nearly always followed by the procession of nurses and the man with the basin and the funnel. Gradually she became a little more aware of her surroundings. She was no longer lying on the floor, but in a sort of wooden manger clamped to the ground in the middle of a cell. Now she had not even a blanket, only a kind of stiff canvas apron, like a piece of sail-cloth, stretched over her. And she was wearing, not a shirt, but a curious enveloping garment, very stiff and rough, that encased her legs and feet and came down over her hands. It had a leather collar, like an animal's, and a belt with a metal ring. Between the visita-

tions of the funnel she dozed and dreamt. Or she
would lie quietly, quite happy to watch, hour after
hour, the play of pearly colours on the piece of
sailcloth. Her name had irrevocably gone, but
whole piece of her past life, people, episodes,
poems, remained embedded in her mind. She
could remember the whole of 'The Mistress of
Vision' and say it over to herself as she lay there.
But if a word had gone, she could not suggest another to fill the gap, unless it was one of those
odd, meaningless words that she found herself
making up now and then.

One night there was a thunderstorm. She was
frightened. The manger had become a little raft;
when she put out her hand she could feel waves
lapping right up to the brim. She had always been
afraid of water in the dark. Now she began to
pray. The door opened and a nurse, with a red
face and pale hair and lashes, peered round the
door, and called to her:

'Rosa Mystica.'

Helen called back:

'Turris Davidica.'

'Turris Eburnea,' called the nurse.

'Domus Aurea,' cried Helen.

And so, turn by turn, they recited the whole of
the Litany of Our Lady.

One day she discovered that, by standing up in

the manger, she could see through a high window, covered with close wire-netting, out into a garden. This discovery gave her great pleasure. In the garden women and nurses were walking; they did not look like real people, but oddly thin and bright, like figures cut out of coloured paper. And she could see birds flying across the sky, not real birds, but bird-shaped kites, lined with strips of white metal that flew on wires. Only the clouds had thickness and depth and looked as clouds had looked in the other world. The clouds spoke to her sometimes. They wrote messages in white smoke on the blue. They would take shape after shape to amuse her, shapes of swans, of feathers, of charming ladies with fluffy white muffs and toques, of soldiers in white busbies.

Once the door of her cell opened and there appeared, not a nurse, but a woman with short, frizzy hair, who wore a purple jumper, a tweed skirt, and a great many amber beads. Helen at once decided that this woman's name was Stella. She had a friendly, silly face, and an upper lip covered with dark down.

'I've brought you a pencil,' she announced suddenly. 'I think you're so sweet. I've seen you from the garden, often. Shall we be friends?'

But before Helen could answer, the woman threw up her head, giggled, shot Helen an odd, sly look, and disappeared. With a sudden, sharp, quite normal horror, Helen thought, 'She's mad.'

She thought of the faces she had seen in the garden, with that same sly, shallow look. There must be other people in the place, then. For the first time, she was grateful for the locked door. She had a horror of mad people, of madness. Her own private horror had always been that she would go mad.

She was feeling quiet and reasonable that day. Her name had not come back to her, but she could piece together some shreds of herself. She recognized her hands; they were thinner and the nails were broken, but they were the hands she had had in the life with Dorothy and Robert and the others. She recognized a birthmark on her arm. She felt light and tired, as if she had recovered from a long illness, but sufficiently interested to ask the nurse who came in:

'What is this place?'

The nurse, who was young and pretty, with coppery hair and green eyes, looked at Helen with pity and contempt. She was kindly, with the ineffable stupid kindliness of nurses.

'I'm not supposed to tell you anything, you know.'

'I won't give you away,' promised Helen. 'What is it?'

'Well! it's a hospital, if you must know.'

'But what *kind* of a hospital?'

'Ah, that'd be telling.'

'What *kind* of a hospital?' persisted Helen.

'A hospital for girls who ask too many questions and have to give their brains a rest. Now go to sleep.'

She shook a playful finger and retreated.

It was difficult to know when the episode of the rubber room took place. Time and place were very uncertain, apt to remain stationary for months, and then to dissolve and fly in the most bewildering way. Sometimes it would take her a whole day to lift a spoon to her mouth; at other times she would live at such a pace that she could see the leaves of the ivy on the garden wall positively opening and growing before her eyes. The only thing she was sure of was that the rubber room came after she had been changed into a salmon and shut up in a little dry, waterless room behind a waterfall. She lay wriggling and gasping, scraping her scales on the stone floor, maddened by the water pouring just beyond the bars that she could not get through. Perhaps she died as a salmon as she had died as a horse, for the next thing she remembered was waking in a small, six-sided room whose walls were all thick bulging panels of grey rubber. The door was rubber-padded too, with a small red window, shaped like an eye, deeply embedded in it. She was lying on the floor, and through the red, a face, stained red too, was watching her and laughing.

She knew without being told, that the rubber room was a compartment in a sinking ship, near the boiler room, which would burst at any minute and scald her to death. Somehow she must get out. She flung herself wildly against the rubber walls as if she could beat her way out by sheer force. The air was getting hotter. The rubber walls were already warm to touch. She was choking, suffocating: in a second her lungs would burst. At last the door opened. They were coming to rescue her. But it was only the procession of nurses and the funnel once more.

The fantasies were not always horrible. Once she was in a cell that was dusty and friendly, like an attic. There were spider-webs and an old ship's lamp on the ceiling. In the lamp was a face like a fox's mask, grinning down at her. She was sitting on a heap of straw, a child of eleven or so, with hair the colour of straw, and an old blue pinafore. Her name was Veronica. With crossed legs and folded arms she sat there patiently making a spell to bring her brother Nicholas safe home. He was flying back to her in a white aeroplane with a green propeller. She could see his face quite clearly as he sat between the wings. He wore a fur cap like a cossack's and a square green ring on his little finger. Enemies had put Veronica in prison, but Nicholas would come to rescue her as he had always come before. She and Nicholas loved each other with a love far deeper and more subtle than any love between husband and wife. She knew at once if he were in pain or danger, even if he were a thousand miles away.

Nicholas came to her window and carried her away. They flew to Russia, and landed on a plain covered with snow. Then they drove for miles in a sledge until they came to a dark pine forest. They walked through the forest, hand in hand, Veronica held close in Nicholas's great fur cape. But at last she was tired, dazed by the silence and the endless trees, all exactly alike. She wanted to sit down in the snow, to sleep.

Nicholas shook her: 'Never go to sleep in the snow, Ronnie, or you will die.'

But she was too tired to listen, and she lay down in the snow that was soft and strangely warm, and fell into an exquisite dreamy torpor. And perhaps she did die in the snow as Nicholas had said, for the next thing she knew was that she was up in the clouds, following a beautiful Indian woman who sailed before her, and sifting snow

61

down on the world through the holes in her pinafore.

Whenever things became too intolerable, the Indian woman would come with her three dark, beautiful sons, and comfort her. She would draw her sweet-smelling yellow veil over Helen and sing her songs that were like lullabies. Helen could never remember the songs, but she could often feel the Indian woman near, when she could not see her, and smell her sweet, musky scent.

She had a strange fantasy that she was Lord of the World. Whatever she ordered came about at once. The walls of the garden outside turned to blue ice that did not melt in the sun. All the doors of the house flew open and the passages were filled with children dressed in white and as lovely as dreams. She called up storms; she drove ships out of their courses; she held the whole world in a spell. Only herself she could not command. When the day came to an end she was tired out, but she could not sleep. She had forgotten the charm, or never known it, and there was no one powerful enough to say to her, 'Sleep.'

She raved, she prayed, but no sleep came. At last three women appeared.

'You cannot sleep unless you die,' they said.

She assented gladly. They took her to a beach and fettered her down on some stones, just under the bows of a huge ship that was about to be launched. One of the three gave a signal. Nothing could stop it now. On it came, grinding the pebbles to dust, deafening her with noise. It passed, slowly, right over her body. She felt every bone crack; felt the intolerable weight on her shoulders, felt her skull split like a shell. But she could sleep now. She was free from the intolerable burden of having to will.

After this she was born and re-born with incredible swiftness as a woman, as an imp, as a dog, and finally as a flower. She was some nameless, tiny bell, growing in a stream, with a stalk as fine as hair and a human voice. The water flowing through her flower throat made her sing all day a little monotonous song, 'Kulallah, Kulallah.' This happy flower-life did not last long. Soon there came a day when the place was filled with nurses who called her 'Helen'. She did not recognize the name as her own, but she began to answer it mechanically as a dog answers a familiar sound.

She began to put on ordinary clothes, clumsily and with difficulty, as if she had only just learned how, and to be taken for walks in a dreary yard; an asphalt-paved square with one sooty plane-tree and a broken bench in the middle. Wearily she would trail round and round between two nurses who polished their nails incessantly as they walked and talked about the dances they had been to. She began to recognize some of her companions in the yard. There was the woman with the beads, the Vitriol woman, and the terrible Caliban girl. The Caliban girl was called Micky. She was tall and rather handsome, but Helen never thought of her except as an animal or a monster, and was horrified when Micky tried to utter human words. Her face was half-beautiful, half-unspeakable, with Medusa curls and great eyes that looked as if they were carved out of green stone. Two long, yellow teeth, like tiger's fangs, grew right down over her lip. She had a queer passion for Helen, who hated and feared her. Whenever she could, Micky would break away from her nurses and try to fondle Helen. She would stroke her hair, muttering, 'Pretty, pretty,' with her deformed mouth. Micky's breath on her cheek was hot and sour like an animal's, her black hair was rough as wire. The reality of Micky was worse than any nightmare; she was shameful, obscene.

The Vitriol woman was far more horrible to look at, but far less repulsive. Helen had heard the nurses whispering how the woman's husband had thrown acid at her. Her face was one raw, red, shining burn, without lid or brow, almost without lips. She always wore a neat black hat and a neat, common blue coat with a fur collar.

Everyone she met she addressed with the same agonized question: 'Have you seen Fred? Where's Fred? Take me to Fred!'

On one of the dirty walls someone had chalked up:

'Baby.'

'Blood.'

'Murder.'

And no one had bothered to wipe it out.

The yard was a horror that seemed to have no place in the world, yet from beyond the walls would come pleasant ordinary noises of motors passing, and people walking and bells ringing. Above the walls, Helen could see a rather beautiful, slender dome, pearl-coloured against the sky, and tipped with a gilt spear. It reminded her of some building she knew very well but whose name, like her own, she had forgotten.

One day, she was left almost alone in the yard. Sitting on the broken bench by the plane-tree was a young girl, weeping. Helen went up to her. She had a gentle, bewildered face; with loose, soft plaits falling round it. Helen went and sat by her and drew the girl's head on to her own shoulder. It seemed years since she had touched another person with affection. The girl nestled against her. Her neck was greenish-white, like privet; when Helen touched it curiously, its warmth and softness were so lovely that tears came into her eyes. The girl was so gentle and defenceless, like some small, confiding animal, that Helen felt a sudden love for her run through all her veins. There was a faint country smell about her hair, like clover.

'I love you,' murmured Helen, hardly knowing what she said.

But suddenly a flock of giggling nurses were upon them with a chatter of:

'Look at this, will you?' and,

'Break away there.'

She never saw the country girl again.

And so day after day went past, punctuated by dreary meals and drearier walks. She lived through each only because she knew that sooner or later Robert must come to fetch her away, and this hope carried her through each night. There were messages from him sometimes, half-glimpsed in the flight of birds, in the sound of a horn beyond the walls, in the fine lines ruled on a blade of grass. But he himself never came, and at last there came a day when she ceased to look for him. She gave up. She accepted everything. She was no longer Helen or Veronica, no longer even a fairy horse. She had become an Inmate.

The Saint

CHILDREN, as you know, are supposed to have a special power of discerning saints. A great many years ago, when I was a child at a convent school, a number of us were certain that we had divined one in our very midst.

The name of the saint was Mother Lucilla Ryan. She was about thirty years old, very beautiful in a way that was both spiritual and witty, and she was dying of consumption.

We came back from our long summer holidays to find that the consumption, which for months had moved stealthily, almost invisibly, had begun to gallop. It was too late to send her abroad to the Order's sanatorium at Montreux. She was to die here, in the community infirmary, among her own friends.

Mother Lucilla had been in direct charge of the Junior School, so that we felt her to be peculiarly *our* saint. The tiny notes she scribbled us now and then, exquisitely written notes pencilled on scraps of squared paper torn from an exercise-book, we slipped reverently into our missals, convinced that one day they would be sought-after relics. Charlotte, I remember, even went to far as to print on hers 'Actual writing of the Blessed Lucilla Ryan'.

We were amazed at her boldness, but we secretly felt that it would be justified.

I think we were just a little disappointed that Mother Lucilla was dying in her bed and not at the stake. Canonization, we knew, was a long and tedious process, and we wanted quick results. Martyrdom, as everyone knows, is the royal road to sainthood, and we would have trusted Mother Lucilla under any torture. Her bravery, indeed, was almost legendary. Some of the Senior School could remember how she had caught her finger in the see-saw one day during recreation. Without so much as a grimace, she had folded her wounded hand in her sleeve and stood for the rest of the hour, directing games as usual, with that odd, delicate smile of hers. Not until she had marshalled the children back indoors did anyone know that the top half of one finger had been torn right away.

It can never be an easy task to succeed a saint, especially in the critical eyes of twenty small girls, but few people could have failed more conspicuously than poor Mother MacDowell. There was nothing to appeal to the most charitable imagination about our new mistress. To begin with, she was very plain; small and stocky, with a red, hard-bitten face and thick, refracting glasses. Through these amazing glasses, her small, dull eyes appeared enormous, like the eyes of an insect.

68

Somehow or other we knew that her father had
gone blind and that her parents had made her
spend an hour every day alone in the dark, so that
if she, too, were to go blind she would be less helpless. Had we heard such a story about Mother
Lucilla, it would be one more legend of her
saintly patience. But it was part of the general un-
fortunateness of Mother MacDowell that everything that happened to her should seem dull, common, and even rather ridiculous. The very tasks
she was given by the community seemed to be
chosen to display her at her worst. Besides looking after us, she was mistress of needlework for
the whole school, though, even with her glasses,
she could hardly see to thread a needle. Her red
hands, speckled with pricks, looked clumsier than
ever, moving stiffly and painfully over the gauzy
linen we were embroidering for altar cloths.
Everything about her was unromantic. Her habit
was the shabbiest in the convent. Her rosary was
broken in three places and mended with wire. She
suffered from titanic colds that made look plainer
than ever. And, to crown all, her Christian name
was Keziah.

We were prepared to receive her with a cold
dislike, but there was something about Mother
MacDowell's attitude to our adored Mother Lucilla that ripened the dislike into hostility. I don't

mean that she ever said anything uncharitable about Mother Lucilla or that she did not encourage us to pray for her. But the sight of any extravagant devotion, and, above all, any mention of the word 'saint', roused her to unwonted anger.

The four-o'clock recreation, when we did not play games, but sat about with our mistress, munching thick slices of bread and jam, was always a time for discussion. I am afraid it was also a favourite time for baiting Mother MacDowell. One afternoon, as we sat round her under the plane-tree on the dusty, stony, Junior School playground, Charlotte said, raising innocent eyes:

'Mother MacDowell, do you think Mother Lucilla is a saint?'

'It is not for us to say who are saints and who are not. That is for God to declare, through the mouth of the Church,' said Mother MacDowell piously.

'But don't you think Mother Lucilla's awfully holy?' persisted Charlotte who had been a great favourite of Mother Lucilla's, if saints can be said to have favourites.

'Only God can know that. We all need infinite mercy. No doubt we shall all have a great many surprises at the Last Day.'

We looked at each other. The five-minute bell rang.

'Come along, Charlotte, eat your bread and jam. You haven't even begun it,' said Mother MacDowell sharply.

'I don't want it,' said Charlotte self-consciously.

'Don't be absurd, child. Be thankful to the dear Lord who sent it you, and eat up your good food.'

'But—Mother——' Charlotte wriggled.

'Well, child?'

'I wanted to do a penance for Mother Lucilla. You said we all needed prayers. So I thought I'd give up my *goûter* for her.'

We gave Charlotte admiring glances. None of us had thought of doing that.

'God does not want penances of that sort,' said Mother MacDowell very decidedly. 'He would far rather that, instead of showing off like that, you made an act of humility and ate your *goûter* like the others. That would be a real penance.'

Charlotte turned crimson and began to eat her bread in small, martyred bites. Although we could not resist a faint pang of pleasure in seeing her scored off, the general feeling was that Mother MacDowell had showed a very mean spirit. A week later, Mother Lucilla died. As a great privilege, we were allowed to see her as she lay among the lilies in the Lady Chapel that had once been a

71

ballroom and that still had gilt garlands of leaves
and little violins on the walls. We filed round the
bier on tiptoe, in our black veils and gloves, passing from hand to hand the heavy silver *asperges*
and clumsily sprinkling drops of holy water on
Mother Lucilla's black habit, that had become
sculptured and unreal like a statue's robe. Not
one of us doubted, as we looked at her lying there,
pale as wax and still smiling, as if she had just been
told some holy secret, that we were looking at a
saint.

The morning she was buried they dressed us in
the white serge uniforms that we wore only on
big feast days. Carrying candles that burnt with a
faint, nearly invisible flame in the May sunlight,
the whole school passed in long ranks under the
alley of limes that led to the nuns' cemetery. At
the graveside we formed a hollow square, with
the younger ones in the centre. Mother Lucilla's
four tall brothers, who were all officers in the
Irish Guards, carried the coffin; the little boys
from the Poor School, transformed into a choir
with white surplices, chirped the 'De Profundis'
like so many sparrows. We peered with respectful
curiosity into the hollow grave. It was lined with
spruce boughs that had a solemn, unforgettable
smell. Father Kelly was praying, in his rich voice
that sounded splendid out of doors, that all the

angels might come to meet her at the doors of heaven; the four tall brothers were paying out the bands of the deal coffin that looked like a soldier's, when the wonderful thing happened. As the nuns intoned the Amen, a white butterfly flew up out of the grave, hung for a minute so that we could all see it, then spiralled away, with a flight as purposeful as a bird's, right up into the blue air.

We looked round curiously. Some of the nuns were gazing up after the butterfly. Mother MacDowell, I noticed, was not one of these. Her red face was bowed and impassive, though the sun danced furiously in her spectacles. But Reverend Mother, who had been weeping a little, lifted her head, and, looking straight at the Junior School, gave us a smile that was positively triumphant. Almost giddy with excitement and happiness, we smiled back. It was a Sign, if ever there was one.

We were rather subdued for the rest of the day. Even poor Mother MacDowell did not find us quite so impossible as usual. At tea-time recreation we gathered round her in quite a friendly way, while the conversation turned quite naturally on saints. But, today, we were careful to mention no names.

Charlotte, sitting astride a branch of the plane-tree, bent down to ask, very politely:

'How long does it take for a saint to get canonized?'

'Many years, my dear child—centuries sometimes.'

'Like the English martyrs,' put in Laura. 'They've only just been done, haven't they, Mother?'

There was a murmur of disappointment. Then someone had a bright thought.

'But what about the Blessed Marie Madeleine Pérot?' said a voice falling over itself with excitement. 'She's not just Blessed, she's Saint now, and I know a girl whose grandmother was at the Sacred Heart when Mother Pérot was Mistress-General, and the grandmother's still alive.'

We sighed with relief.

'But it's awfully difficult, isn't it, Mother?' said Laura the pessimist. 'There's the Devil's Advocate, and they've got to prove major miracles worked by direct intercession and all that, haven't they?'

Mother MacDowell gave a small, dour smile at this—very different from the angelic smile of Mother Lucilla.

'It's not the miracles that matter so much, my dear. They're only outward signs. There have been big saints who worked no miracles and little saints who worked many. No, what matters is that the person should have attained heroic sanctity on this earth.'

Heroic sanctity? It sounded very difficult indeed. We were quiet for a minute, knitting our brows. Then one by one we remembered Mother Lucilla's severed finger. If that was not heroic sanctity, what was? But suddenly our thoughts were turned violently back to earth. There was a noise of breaking wood, a shrill scream and a crash. Charlotte had fallen off her perch in the plane-tree and was lying on the stones. We drew back, frightened. Mother MacDowell hesitated for a second before she advanced and picked Charlotte up. Then she sat down with Charlotte on her lap while the rest of us stood in a gaping circle. Charlotte's knee bled in streams; Mother MacDowell's habit was already wet and shining. But it was at the nun's face and not at Charlotte's cut knee that we were all looking. For Mother MacDowell had turned from red to a dreadful greenish white. We knew what it was—she was one of those people who cannot bear the sight of blood. But there was no pity in us that day; we all remembered Mother Lucilla, who never flinched at the sight of blood, not even her own. But, to do justice to Mother MacDowell, she managed to control herself. Her lips were trembling, she could not speak, but she produced her coarse white handkerchief as big as table napkin, and began to wipe away the dirt from the cut knee. Finally, having roughly bandaged Charlotte, who behaved with a stoicism worthy of Mother Lucilla herself, she told off four of us to take our wounded friend to the infirmary. We waited in interested silence while the infirmary sister unwound the handkerchief. The bleeding had entirely stopped. The sister examined the leg carefully; then she began to laugh. 'Why, you little sillies, there's not even a cut. Run along, Charlotte. There's nothing the matter with you—nothing except a *dirty* knee, that is.'

It was pefectly true. There were specks of brown gravel on Charlotte's knee, and that was all. There was not even a spot of blood on the handkerchief.

But when the five of us were in the garden again, Charlotte beckoned us round her, with an air of great solemnity.

'Swear you won't tell—or, rather, don't swear—promise, because it's something holy.'

We promised eagerly.

'Well, you know there *was* a cut on my knee—you all saw how it bled. And it hurt awfully.'

We nodded.

'Well, when Mother MacDowell began to wipe it with her handkerchief, there was suddenly an

76

awful pain in it, as if it had been burnt or something—and then I just *knew* the cut wasn't there any more.'

'But, Charlotte,' I gasped, 'if that really happened—it was a——'

She seized my hand.

'I know,' she said feverishly, 'it was—a miracle.'

We stared at her with awe-struck admiration.

But Laura, the rationalist, said:

'Who worked it then? Someone's got to work a miracle. Did you pray to anyone?'

'Well—not exactly. But I had my rosary—the one that touched Her—in my pocket.'

It was quite enough for us. Mother Lucilla was as good as canonized in our eyes.

'Promise not to tell yet,' implored Charlotte.

We promised. And we certainly kept the letter of our promise. But, back on the playground, someone asked Mother MacDowell in an off-hand kind of way:

'How big does a major miracle have to be? Would it be a major miracle if a broken arm got set by itself? Or if an awfully deep cut suddenly healed up of its own accord?'

But Mother MacDowell turned fiery red and snapped out: 'That is enough talk about miracles, children. You are all thoroughly over-excited. You will talk French at supper and go to bed half an hour earlier if this goes on.'

We hastily quitted the subject of miracles. Just as we were forming into file to go back to the house, one of the Senior School came running towards Mother MacDowell. She stopped, fumbled in her pocket, and produced a rosary.

'I found this in the Junior School benches, Mother. Does it belong to any of your children?'

The rosary was of the kind rich parents give their children for First Communion presents; carved amethyst beads threaded on a gold chain. Mother MacDowell held it up by the tip of her fingers; had it been any secular object, one would have said she held it disdainfully.

'And whose is this?' she asked. 'I seem to have seen——'

But Charlotte was already skipping forward to claim her property.

I suppose it must be thirty or forty years since it all happened. Laura is a Carmelite nun, and Charlotte, who married a millionaire, and a Protestant at that, is a grandmother. I might even have forgotten all about it if I had not read in my *Universe* yesterday that the Canonization of the Blessed Keziah MacDowell had just been ratified by the Holy See.

Aunt Rose's Revenge

MY Aunt Rose was a figure of considerable fascination to me in my childhood. For one thing, she lived in Vienna. Her sister, my Aunt Lily, also lived in Vienna, but she did not appeal to my imagination as much as Aunt Rose. I knew only one fact about Aunt Lily: that she had a weak chest, a thing which was neither unusual nor interesting. But I knew two facts about Aunt Rose and found them both impressive. One was that, as a child, she had crushed a finger in a doll's mangle and had to have part of it amputated. The other was that she had a remarkably violent temper.

In our attic at home there stood for many years an old hip-bath with a large black patch where the enamel had been burnt off. It was known as 'Aunt Rose's Revenge', and the story was that my Aunt Rose had deliberately set fire to it after an argument with my mother. When I was very young I had a confused idea that this hip-bath somehow *was* Aunt Rose, and I paid many secret visits to it with feelings of awe, admiration, and pity. If anything, my admiration increased when I realized that Aunt Rose had not been turned into the hip-bath as a punishment for her wickedness.

I felt that only a very powerful and splendid being could have done anything as naughty as that and escaped retribution.

Aunt Rose's was the first grown-up handwriting I was able to read. It was very large, and each letter was painstakingly formed so that it looked like a glorified version of my own. My mother said this was because of the awkward way she had to hold her pen; it was the forefinger of her right hand that was mutilated. Twice a year I received gay cards, always written in violet ink, wishing me alternately '*Fröhliche Ostern*' and '*Fröhliche Weinachten*'. These gave me a delicious sense of being cosmopolitan and practically bi-lingual. As time went on and I acquired as well various dolls in *Dirndl* and *Lederhosen*, not to mention a cowbell from Salzburg, I began to feel I knew Austria very well indeed. At school I managed to imply, without actually saying so, that I had spent a good deal of time there.

Once she sent me a snapshot of herself rowing on a lake with a very elegant woman and a foreign-looking but quite sensibly dressed child of my own age. On the back she had written: 'I am having a most delightful holiday with my dear friend the Countess von Schüttelheim and her daughter Trude. I wish you could be here.' Since Aunt Rose's plain, fierce face was almost hidden by a large hat and she seemed to be wearing the same sort of clothes as the Countess, I passed this round at supper saying carelessly: 'I jolly well wish I were there. The Schüttelheim's *Schloss* is simply heavenly, and Trude's lots more fun than most Austrian girls.' After that Aunt Rose frequently sent me snapshots of herself and always in the most distinguished company, but I seldom passed them round. Too often on the back there would be a word in that painfully legible writing which might give a clue to something I had never told even my most reliable friends. Aunt Rose did not live in Vienna for a private fancy; she lived there because she was an English governess.

During the 1914–18 war, the letters in purple ink arrived only at long intervals and by devious routes. Only one snapshot arrived: a blurred picture of Aunt Lily's grave almost hidden by the censor's rubber stamp. We did not hear of her death till six months after it occurred. 'Dearest Lily got pneumonia going out in the snow to give her lessons: her shoes were *ersatz*, and no more use than cardboard. I could not take care of her as she needed. Our Austrian friends were *most* kind (we have never been penalized: there is no hatred of the *English* here), but even the richest have only the bare minimum of food and fuel. People sell fur coats and pearl necklaces for sacks

of potatoes. We had, of course, no milk or butter.
She wanted tea so much, but naturally there was
none to be had. I could only give her the infusion
of dried blackberry leaves we use instead. It was
impossible to keep her warm: there was nothing
to put in the grate but balls of newspaper and wet
twigs I picked up in the Belvedere Park.'

Vienna seemed very far away in those years.
My parents told me now and then, as news leaked
through, what hardships Aunt Rose must have
endured through those terrible winters. 'Poor
dear Rose,' my mother said. 'How she used to
grumble in the old days!' She smiled. 'The hip-
bath. It was something to do with the way cook
made coffee. And now, when she has such dreadful
things to put up with, she hardly complains at all.'

Then the rare letters began to have a new re-
frain. 'Even when this *fearful* war is over, will my
beloved Wien ever be the same? I begin to think
of England as the Promised Land. It is my dream
to come and see you all if the happy days of Peace
ever return.'

The happy days of peace returned, but Aunt
Rose did not realize her dream of visiting us. In
1918, I calculate that she must have been fifty-five:
she had been a governess since she was seventeen,
the age I was myself when the war ended. She had
lived thriftily, managing to put by a little every

year; since the holiday of the hip-bath episode in 1900, she had denied herself the pleasure of a visit to England. Her sister Lily had stayed with us in the summer of 1913; six years later Aunt Rose wrote: 'How I scolded poor Lil for being so extravagant, but as it turned out, she was the wise one.' The war had made a large hole in their savings: the inflation reduced the remainder to little more than waste paper. 'A hatbox full of notes to buy a loaf! People go shopping wheeling barrows of paper money. I thank God that dear Lil was spared from knowing that everything we had put by in over thirty years was only worth a few shillings. When she was dying, she kept saying: "You'll have my savings, darling, as well as your own. You'll be able to go home and perhaps buy yourself a little cottage." She would have been too delicate to start all over again as I must now. I am keeping on our tiny flat. Many friends have wished to share it with me. But, though I can ill afford it, I prefer to be independent. As you know, I have always been *extremely* independent by nature.'

Like Queen Victoria, Aunt Rose was given to underlining, and she had underlined 'extremely' twice. Nine years later I proved that she was fully justified in doing so.

. . . . . .

In the summer of 1928 I decided to spend my three weeks' leave from the office in Vienna. Aunt Rose had been begging me to visit her for years. As soon as I announced the actual date, I was deluged with purple-ink letters. 'Why not come earlier? The season really *ends* in May. *All* the society people will be away. You will even miss the Opera.' I wrote more than once explaining that I was not a free agent, and it must be August or not at all. She ignored all my explanations as well as inquiries for actual figures of the cost of living. In the last letter of this cross-purpose correspondence she wrote: 'We who live here have to worry about expense. But for you, with *English* money, it is *quite* unnecessary. You will find Vienna *ludicrously* cheap. As my little flat will not be at all what you are accustomed to, I have booked you a nice room in a very *bequem* hotel in the Kärnthnerstrasse.'

I arrived at the *Erzherzogin Anna* very late at night. It was as comfortable as possible, but I doubted if I should find it ludicrously cheap. It had a large staff and that air of sober richness which suggested the worst. A glance at the price list bound in gilded leather confirmed my fears. My room alone, without bath, would cost 35 *schillings* a night—a pound in English money; even at that late hour I had already encountered

84

at least three people who would have to be tipped. I suspected that Aunt Rose had lived so long abroad that she had come to share the prevalent belief that all English tourists are wealthy. To-morrow I would tell her the real state of the case and ask her to suggest somewhere cheaper. Meanwhile, I might as well enjoy my one night of extravagance.

When I came down in the morning, the proprietor and his entire family were lined up to greet me. They were charming people. My hand was kissed with the same courtly grace by all the men from the grandfather to eight-year-old Heinzl; a carnation was pinned to my frock. I was assured that the gracious niece of their dear and highly respected Miss Little had only to express a wish for it to be gratified. But, weak as my German was, I understood quite clearly that I was not being offered free hospitality. My aunt seemed to have impressed on them that the English were too proud to accept even a small reduction on the tariff. I had not the courage to say that the *Erzherzogin Anna* was beyond my means and that I should probably be leaving that day.

· · · · · ·

I made my way to the address in the Belvedere-gasse, rather struck by the respect Aunt Rose seemed to have inspired in the Drücke family. Was it possible that she was not so poor as we supposed her to be since the war? I climbed flights of dark stone steps, past several landings on which stood unemptied dustbins, till I reached her flat, *Tür* 10. A fierce-looking elderly lady, carrying a chipped coffee-pot, opened the door. She gave me a glance of the utmost suspicion, then flung out her arms and cried: 'Elizabeth! *Liebchen!* At last!'

We went into a bare little sitting-room with linoleum on the floor and one or two threadbare rugs. It was furnished with three lame wickerwork chairs, a table, a few potted plants, and innumerable photographs. The August sun poured in, showing up the layers of dust and revealing every pouch and wrinkle on Aunt Rose's face; that plain, angry face I had known from photographs since my childhood. Though she was now in her sixties, she looked elderly rather than old. Her short, stout body was defiantly upright, and there was not a thread of grey in her bird's nest of dull, soft brown hair. She wore, in spite of the heat, a dress of faded black serge and an ancient lack-lustre moleskin stole that smelt of mothballs. In spite of myself, I could not help looking surreptitiously for the missing finger. She had learnt to conceal it so cleverly that, though she gesti-

culated all the time she talked, it was several minutes before I saw that her right forefinger ended
below the knuckle. When I did, it hardly dis-
turbed me, for by that time I had become fasci-
nated by Aunt Rose's hands. Time and hardship
had played their cruellest tricks on her face and
figure, but had left her hands intact. They were
small, white, and smooth, with the plump yet taper-
ing fingers you see in Victorian Books of Beauty.

After the rapturous greetings and the family
messages, I delicately broached, as I sipped my
coffee from a cracked cup, the subject of moving
to another hotel. A gleam—I swear it was red—
came into Aunt Rose's eyes, and the pincer-lines
round her mouth deepened.

'Impossible. *Quite* impossible. It would give
great offence to the Drückes. They are very
dear friends of mine. Besides, it is a very old
family. Before the war, they lived like princes.
Like princes, *verstehst Du*? Now, like so many of
our best people who have lost their money, they
have gone into business. They would suppose
my English niece, of whom they have heard so
much, did not find the hotel good enough.'

I tried to explain that the hotel was too good;
that I had only a limited sum for my three weeks;
that my London flat had to be kept going while I
was away; that frankly I could not afford . . .

Aunt Rose broke in superbly: 'Naturally I have not asked what they charge. I should not be so tactless. I can assure you you will be given excellent value for whatever you may pay. And, as *my* niece, particular attention.'

'Oh, I know, Aunt Rose. They said so. They were most awfully kind to me because I was your niece.'

'They think the world of me,' she said simply. 'All my old friends and pupils do.' She indicated the ranks of photographs that might have illustrated an article on 'Four Generations of Fashion'. There were women in fringes and bustles, in enormous hats and 'Princess' frocks, in the Dolly Vardens and bunchy panniers I could remember myself, down to a few contemporary shingles, hip-length jumpers, and knee-high skirts. There were young men, too; some in student caps, some in the white uniform of the Imperial Guard.

'Look at them closer, if you wish,' said Aunt Rose. It was a command and I obeyed. I wondered if a slim youth in Tyrolean costume with edelweiss embroidered on his braces could possibly be Herr Drücke; there was a decided likeness to the little boy Heinzl.

'The grandfather, not the father,' she explained. 'He was one of my very first pupils. I prepared him for one of the diplomatic examinations. I was

88

only a girl myself at the time, so it was not considered correct for me to give him lessons alone. His sister's chaperone always had to sit in the room with us.'

Nearly all the photographs were signed affectionately and exuberantly: 'With grateful affection', 'With everlasting regard', 'From an idle, but devoted pupil'.

'Some of the most famous names in Austria,' Aunt Rose assured me, and began to give me details of intricate family histories. I listened for several minutes. Then, hesitantly, I returned to the attack.

'You see, Aunt Rose, my room . . . it's a lovely room, of course . . . alone costs over a pound . . .'

'*Of course* they have given you one of their best rooms. I should be exceedingly displeased if they had not.' My aunt took a deep breath and expelled it through her nostrils with a sound like an inverted sniff. I recognized the danger signs. My mother had said: 'If Rose tosses her head and snorts, go carefully.'

'They've given me a beautiful room,' I said hastily. 'And they have been simply charming. I don't know how to thank you for having arranged everything so perfectly.'

The sound of a lavender-woman's song, a harsh haunting cadence, almost like *cante flamenco*, came up through the closed window. I did not want to spend the whole of my first morning in Vienna in Aunt Rose's sitting-room.

'You'll come out and have some lunch with me, won't you?' I asked. 'I'm longing for you to show me something of Vienna.'

'Vienna!' She almost sang the word in her soft, light voice. Her voice was almost as incongruous as her hands. It was a young girl's voice, occasionally breaking into a musical giggle. She spoke English with no accent, but with the Viennese lilt, pausing now and then to find the right word. After nearly fifty years away from her own country, German came more naturally to her. 'My beloved *Wien*. If only you could have seen it at its best, in the days of Franz Josef. Naughty girl, why did you leave it so late?' She shook her undamaged forefinger at me.

'But, Aunt Rose, I was only a child in the great days.'

'*Ach*, I forgot. I am getting old and *dumm*. For a minute I thought you were Helen.'

I realized with a shock that my mother must have been about my age when Aunt Rose last saw her.

'*Die Zeit ist so grausam*,' she sighed. 'You know German, Lisa?'

'A very little. Time is so cruel?'

'Splendid. Stay for six months, and I will give you perfect German. I am an *excellent* teacher. Everyone says so.'

'I know. But, alas, I've only three weeks.'

She snorted.

'Everyone should know German. It is ridiculous not to stay now you are here. Think of the advantage if ever you had to earn your own living. I shall write to your mother tomorrow.'

I reminded her that the reason I could not stay was precisely because I *was* earning my own living.

'My stupid memory! Of course, you have a post on a newspaper. Very well paid, I hope.'

'They don't pay me badly. But living in London is expensive, so you see . . .'

'Then you will find Vienna extremely cheap,' she cut in triumphantly. 'Of course, living on Austrian money, it is not at all cheap for us. Imagine, they have just put up the rent of my flat. It will work out to ten English pounds a year. I complained *strongly* to my landlord. But he is adamant.'

The *Erzherzogin Anna* looked like costing me ten English pounds a week. My salary was fifteen. But it seemed indecent to mention it. I sympathized guiltily about her rent, and implored her to put on her hat and come out.

She assumed a weatherbeaten moleskin toque
to match her scarf, an umbrella, and a crocodile
handbag that must have cost a good deal in 1912.

'My friend the Baroness Launerstahl gave it to
me,' she said happily. 'She broke the pretty little
mirror in it the first day she had it. *Die arme* Hed-
wig, she was so superstitious that she made me a
present of it.'

.   .   .   .   .

We went out into the hot, sunlit street. I was
very willing to saunter at Aunt Rose's pace, admiring the pale-golden buildings, the green spires,
the flower stalls, all the sights and sounds of a new
city. But, before we had gone many yards, she
shook her umbrella imperiously at a taxi.

'It is so much more pleasant to drive, *nicht*?' she
said. 'I will tell him to take us round the Ring.'

We drove round the Ring. At intervals my
Aunt banged on the window and shouted '*Lang-
sam!*' till we settled at the pace of a royal procession. As we drove, she talked of the old days.

'I can remember seeing the Empress Elizabeth,
your namesake, riding here in the early mornings.
The most beautiful woman you ever saw. You do
not see women like that now, even in Vienna. So
distinguished, so *apart*. She used to gallop like
the wind, with the long skirt of her habit stream-

92

ing behind her. The escort could hardly keep up with her; she rode like a Valkyrie. They say she used to have herself sewn into those famous riding-habits . . . she had the most elegant figure in the world . . . so that they should fit like her own skin. Very proud, she was. Very *temperamentvoll*. Her ladies in waiting used to shake in their shoes sometimes. She had almost a mania about her wonderful hair; I forget how many brush-strokes it had to have every day. There was always a white sheet spread under her chair, and if there was one hair on that sheet, she boxed the maid's ears.'

I ventured to suggest this was rather unfair to the maid but Aunt Rose rounded on me.

'She was an Empress, *nicht*? And an Empress who had had terrible tragedy in her life? Is it surprising she should have her little whims and caprices? I'm sure the girl was proud to have her ears boxed by *such* a woman!'

We must have driven for an hour. It was exceedingly pleasant; it was also exceedingly expensive. Eventually I said I was sure she must be hungry. I was beginning to wonder if I had enough on me for lunch after paying the taxi, and suggested that we should eat at the hotel. But Aunt Rose said she was sure I should like to lunch at Mittelheim's, and gave her order to the driver.

Mercifully she allowed me to stop and cash a traveller's cheque.

'Mittelheim's is not so world-famous as Sacher's,' she explained. 'But Sacher's will be full of those dreadful Germans. Ten thousand of them in Vienna this week, and all this talk of *Anschluss*. What a ridiculous notion! Everyone knows the Austrians hate the Germans. Mittelheim's would not let them in: it is very exclusive. I lunched here with Gräfin von Kleidenriede in the old days.'

As I studied the menu, I made rapid calculations. The prices were formidable, but the food sounded delicious, and if anyone ever deserved a treat, it was Aunt Rose. We would have one glorious day: tomorrow I really would have to explain . . .

'You had better have *Paprikahuhn*, Lisa. It is a typical Viennese dish. They used to do it so well here.'

'Splendid. Would you like it too?'

She frowned at the menu.

'I should like chicken, but I eat only boiled chicken. Herr Ober!'

The head waiter, who looked like a cavalry officer, advanced majestically.

'I see no boiled chicken on the menu,' said Aunt Rose.

94

'No, gracious lady. But no doubt it could be arranged.'

'Good. Perhaps you will be so kind as to send for the chef. I have to be *most* careful what I eat. I wish to explain exactly how I like my chicken cooked.'

I stared at Aunt Rose with alarm and admiration. Admiration won. I thought myself rather sophisticated, but never in London, Paris, or Madrid had I dared to send for the chef. The restaurant was full of elegant men and women meekly eating what Mittelheim's offered on a long and varied list. I had taken a table in a darkish corner, snobbishly supposing that Aunt Rose might feel a little embarrassed in her faded serge and ancient moleskin.

The chef arrived. The two had a long conversation in German too technical for me to follow. I could see, however, that my aunt was winning easily on points.

When the chef had retired with great deference, she said:

'So typical of Vienna. Everyone is so obliging. It is our famous *gemütlichkeit*. They have such respect for the English. It does not matter if one is old and shabby. They know an English *lady* when they see one.'

During the very long interval before the boiled

chicken arrived my aunt told me how she had first come to Vienna as a girl of eighteen.

'You don't remember your Grandpapa Little. He died when you were a baby. Your mother must have told you how he came back from playing billiards, bent down to take his boots off, and psst! he was dead. That was how he liked things to happen. He was a very autocratic, impatient old gentleman. There were four of us girls. He did not see himself keeping us for the rest of his life. So he picked the two he thought likely to marry: your mother—she was very pretty—and your Auntie Jan, who was so lively, and kept them at home. He had a little money from his wife's estate, and he bought himself an annuity. Then he told your Aunt Lily and myself that we were to be governesses; not in England, because he would not have considered it correct, but abroad. I was the elder, so I was packed off first. He bought me clothes and a little canvas trunk— I have it now—and escorted me himself to Vienna, where one of his old friends had found me a post. I remember so well the very last afternoon I spent with my father, though it is nearly fifty years ago. He said, "My dear Rose, there is no reason why, if you behave yourself, you should not have a perfectly comfortable life." Then he put a five-pound note into my hand. I had never had so much money in my life. "This is the last actual money you will ever receive from me, my dear, so it is not to be loosely squandered. But do not think I have made no provision for you in case of actual want. I have something most interesting to show you." We walked a very long way till we came to a house in a rather dreary quarter. We were shown into a room where there were a dozen very old ladies, very shabbily dressed, sitting playing patience or knitting. I was eighteen, remember. As we left the house he said, "Now, my dear Rose, you need have no fears for the future. As long as I live I shall order my bankers to pay an annual subscription of a guinea to this excellent institution for Distressed Governesses." '

.   .   .   .   .

By the time the chicken arrived, I had made a series of mental readjustments. I decided I could stay the course for a week. At the end of that time, an urgent telegram would summon me back to London. But, for that week, Aunt Rose and I were going to live on the scale she expected of me. I thought of the blackberry-leaf tea, of Aunt Lily dying in the room with the grate filled with balls of newspaper, of the tramps through the snow in cardboard shoes, of the hatboxes full of useless paper money.

The chef reverently uncovered a copper cas-
serole containing a whole boiled chicken on a bed
of rice that smelt exquisitely of unknown herbs,
Aunt Rose shook her left forefinger at him.

'You have been a very long time,' she said
superbly. 'I trust that does not mean it is not a
young bird. If it is tough or if the rice is over-
cooked, my English niece and I will never come
here again.'

The Exile

WE sat in the dusty and nearly deserted refectory of an obscure provincial college. The prints of Caxton and Sir Thomas More, the peasant pots of wrinkled daffodils did little to convince me that we were not stranded in the refreshment room of a provincial railway station.

Sad men in Norfolk jackets dropped in at intervals, poured themselves out cups of strong tea, drank them hastily, and departed, as if to catch imaginary trains. A waitress peeled off the checked cloths and exposed the tables in their iron nakedness; the plain, unvarnished clock ticked on and on, the scum settled in my half-empty cup, and still Miss Hislop talked.

She was not young. Brown hair, greying at the roots, was bobbed unevenly round her boldly marked, sallow face. As she talked, she twisted a strand of it round a short, knotty finger. Her brown eyes were very restless; like old pearls, they were dimmed as if someone had breathed on them, and there was a white ring round the iris.

'You don't think it awful cheek of me asking

you here like this? Did I tell you in my letter that I was a Catholic? Well, I am. Became one six years ago. Now I'm going to shock you. I haven't been to church for eighteen months. But I believe it all . . . all the dogma, I mean. Only I don't hold with being holy in the world. People who are holy in the world get a bit freakish I always think. No, I want to be a nun, and, if I can't be a nun, I'd rather be a big sinner. Does that shock you? But the way Catholics treat me always makes me behave bad. It's a sort of free-masonry the born and bred ones have, a way that they look at each other when there's a convert in the room, that gets me. And then a devil gets into me and I just have to play them up. Do you understand?

'Have I always wanted to be a nun? Yes, ever since I was nine years old. Long before I was a Catholic or even an Anglo-Catholic. I wanted terribly to go into an Anglo-Catholic sisterhood. I lived in one of their houses for a long time. And there was a nun there called Sister Monica. I loved that woman . . . yes, really loved, if you know what I mean. But the Mother Prioress came between us, and I wasn't allowed to see her. I suffered dreadfully . . . oh, agonies. Ten years it was before I got over Sister Monica. When I became a Catholic, it was because of St. Theresa of

the Child Jesus . . . the one of Lisieux who's a
saint now. I think I only became a Catholic because I wanted to enter Carmel. Well, they were
awfully sweet to me at Carmel—at least Sister
Prisca was—but they kept shilly-shallying about
letting me try my vocation. And then I suppose
I got mad again; anyway, I started to do silly
things that got me into trouble with my parish
priest. A martinet he was, so I wouldn't go to
confession to him, but went to the younger one,
his assistant. Father Roger his name was. I liked
him . . . yes, I *did* like him, but don't misunder-
stand me and think there was anything sexy in it,
because there wasn't. You know what Catholics
are . . . they make a fuss if you so much as look at
anything in trousers. Anyway, the parish priest
got annoyed, and said I wasn't to help Father
Roger with the choir or anything. And I got
miserable and jealous because there was another
woman, and *she* was allowed to help him, and I
didn't see why *I* should be shut out. So, just in a
spirit of pure devilry, I *did* run after Father Roger.
But it was the parish priest's fault . . . he *made* me.
And then he wrote me a beast of a letter. Well, I
saw red then. I did an awful thing . . . really awful . . . a fearful sin. Are you sure you won't be
shocked? Dare I tell you?'

I nodded. Miss Hislop put her face very close to

mine, while with one finger she stirred a crumb of
cake round and round her saucer.

'I stole the Blessed Sacrament,' she whispered,
'I felt I wanted to hurt God, and so I took Him
away. I don't know what I meant to do. I went
to Communion and straight out of the Church
with It in my mouth. Then I went home and took
out the Host and laid It on the table in my digs. I
meant to do something awful with It . . . really
sacrilegious like Black Magic. And then somehow I couldn't. I felt a peculiar sort of tenderness
towards It as if It were a child. I wouldn't have
hurt It for the world. I wanted to keep It always
there with me. Don't you think that proves that
there *is* something there . . . not just bread like
the Protestants think? Well, I put It in a box
with my rosary, and I went back to the church
and made my confession . . . to Father Roger.
But he couldn't give me absolution. They
can't, you know, for a real big sin like that
. . . it has to come from Rome. Well, I had to
bring back the Host. . . . I was sorry, I'd got so
tender towards It . . . and I don't know what
Father Roger did with It . . . ate It or burnt It I
suppose.

'Did I get my absolution? Yes, months after.
But, of course, that put me right back with Carmel. The Mother Prioress interfered, just like the

other one did with Sister Monica, and I wasn't allowed to see Sister Prisca for a whole year. That made me mad again, and I stopped going to church. You see, I only cared for the real old mystic side of it, and you don't get that by going to church and just being an ordinary Catholic. And I'd seen that sort of wonderful spiritual content in Sister Prisca, and that was what I wanted. I knew I'd get it in Carmel and nowhere else, though there are some things in the Carmelite rule that I find it jolly hard to swallow, and I never did believe in cheese as a staple article of diet. But that's neither here nor there.

'I was pretty defiant as I told you, and I didn't care much what happened,' Miss Hislop went on. 'And when I'm in that mood . . . hope I don't shock you . . . I use the most dreadful bad language. I was working here in the college at the time, and on the eve of Saint Theresa I asked Rowlandson (she's a Catholic on the secretarial side here) to have tea with me. I ordered a special tea, but she wouldn't come. Said it was a fast-day, which I knew very well it wasn't, and I was furious. I lost my temper and said, "Damn you, in the devil's name I curse you." That very evening she was knocked down by a lorry and broke both her legs. Well, she's one of the superstitious sort, and she would have it that it was my curse that did it. So she actually wrote to my director (I'd changed over to a Jesuit by now) and asked him to exorcize me because she was sure I was possessed by a devil. And would you believe it, he *did*. I was so furious that I sent him a post card saying: "Thanks for the exorcism; hope it does some good", and, of course, that put me in bad with the Jesuits, too.'

     •   •   •   •

'Well, after a time, they came round a bit at Carmel because I said I was sorry, and they let me see Sister Prisca. Before I'd always seen her with a veil over her face, but not behind the grille, but this time she was behind the curtain, and I couldn't look at her—only hear her voice. That got my goat again, so I made a scene right there in the parlour, and the Mother Prioress turned me out. Well, I've fairly battered at the doors of Carmel since then, but they won't let me in. I wrote to the Bishop, be *he* won't help me. So the only thing is to go to Rome and speak to the Holy Father, like my patron St. Theresa of Lisieux did. I'd got a little money saved, but it wasn't enough, and I've been gambling on horses during the flat-racing season to try to make a bit more, but now it's all gone. So now, if I can get leave from here, I'm going to walk from Marseilles to Rome to see him. I can wangle a place at a canonization ceremony from a Tertiary I know, and I'll make a scene right there in St. Peter's so he'll *have* to listen to me. Funny, isn't it? I haven't said my prayers for six months, yet I'm simply crazy to get into Carmel. Yet I've done everything I could to play them up and annoy them. Once when things were going pretty well, but I thought Sister Prisca had been a bit huffy with me, I told them about a sort of sexy experience I had. Oh, it was nothing, really. But for once I made some sort of impression on a man, and he, well, he made me a certain sort of advances, if you know what I mean. Nothing came of it, of course, but he was really quite keen, though I know I'm not the sort that attracts the opposite sex. But my poor nuns got dreadfully hot and bothered about it. They're a little abnormal about those things, don't you think? But that's the life I want . . . the real old medieval thing . . . mystical substitution and all that.'

She paused at last.

'I must go,' I said.

'Righty-ho,' said Miss Hislop, brightly. '*Jolly* decent of you to have come.'

She gathered up the remains of the walnut cake and stowed them away in a paper bag.

'Come and see my den first,' she invited.

We walked through long, empty, gas-lit corridors and down a flight of stone steps until we came to a small office crammed with files and littered with yellowed back numbers of *The Times*. On the desk lay a bottle of aspirin and a book called 'The Mystery of the Scented Death'.

Suddenly she turned up the gas that hung over the desk and struck an attitude beside it, throwing back her head and jutting out her chin.

'Tell me, do I remind you of anyone? My profile, I mean.'

I studied the curved nose, the receding forehead, the thrust-forward chin, but no resemblance suggested itself.

'Funny,' she said cheerfully. 'Look again. So many people have remarked on it.'

Still I shook my head.

'But I'll get it in a minute,' I hoped.

For the third time she adjusted her profile against the white shade of the gas, straining back her throat till the sinews stood out.

'How about *Dante*?' asked Miss Hislop.

'Of course!' I said weakly.

Strangers

WHEN the telephone bell had first jarred on the warm, intent silence of the third rubber, Mrs. Ferraby had refused to answer. 'It's sure to be a wrong number. That will make the fourth this week.' But it went on whirring with a harsh insistence until Mrs. Ferraby had to give in. Dropping her cards, the first good ones she had held that afternoon, she took the telephone from its pink-silk tabernacle and listened irritably.

'Yes . . . Mrs. Ferraby speaking. . . . I can't hear. Would you talk a little louder please? . . . Your voice is so faint.'

The unknown voice at the other end was a woman's. It began to speak slowly, with a pause between each word:

'Can you hear now? I am speaking from a long distance. This is the Cottage Hospital, Nettlefold, and I am the Matron. I am afraid I have some bad news for you. Your husband has met with an accident in his car, and he is here. . . . No, not the worst. He is knocked about, of course. I have every hope we shall pull him through. Do you think you could get over here tonight? I can give you a room. There is a train from Weybridge at six forty-five. I will send a car to meet you at Nettlefold Station.'

All her life Joan Ferraby had had a name for being competent and level-headed. Habit did not desert her now. Quietly and composedly she dismissed her bridge-party, extended a pale cheek to each member, promised to telephone the next day. She dressed with her usual care, rejecting the grey suede gloves she had worn that morning for a fresher pair, settling her honey-coloured hair in two symmetrical wings under her small felt hat. At school Joan Ferraby had been nicknamed 'The Princess'. Dressing, to her, was more of a public duty than a private pleasure. Her clothes were always immaculate, always unexciting. She had read in a book of Father Benson's that to be the best-dressed woman in any assembly may be a vocation, and had applied it to herself. She dressed to please her husband; to prove that one may be comely and a Catholic. For Mrs. Ferraby had very little vanity. Her honey-coloured hair, her fine milky skin, and neat little features could always ensure her being called a good-looking woman, but she refused to darken her light lashes or redden her pale mouth. At nineteen, when Jim Ferraby had married her, she had looked romantically young, like a Hans Anderson heroine. At thirty, her beauty still clear, still smooth, was touched with frost. Women adored her as they had done all her life. Men envied Jim Ferraby his wife, loved her temperately and married her antithesis.

The journey was cold and uncomfortable. She could not settle down to read. Every other minute she glanced at the square platinum watch that Jim had given her for Christmas. For the first time in her life, she found herself speculating about her fellow-travellers. That woman in the corner with the red, anxious face under her dusty velvet hat—a dreadful hat like a pancake—was she, too, answering some tragic call? Joan hoped not. Grief should be dignified. She raised her chin and pinched her lips a little. The man opposite lowered his paper and stared at her. She turned away and pretended to look out of the window, though she could see nothing but the raindrops quivering and sliding on the glass. Miserably, she counted drop after drop.

At last she made out the name Nettlefold on the station lamps.

A young nurse was there to meet her.

'Matron sent me. She is so sorry she won't be there herself to receive you. She's had to go out; a very urgent case. But she will see you directly she comes in.'

'Is he very badly hurt?' Joan asked.

'We must hope for the best, Matron says. I'm afraid he won't know you. He's quite gone off, you know. But he may come round any minute, and we thought you'd like to be there. It upsets them so, finding themselves among strangers.'

'You have a lot of cases like this, then?'

'Nearly every day, Mrs. Ferraby. We're just near that bad corner, you know. I've seen them come in looking a lot worse than your hubby, and be as spry as anything in a day or two.'

'Is he very bad?'

'Well, he's a good deal knocked about. No bones broken as far as we can see. We've had to bandage his poor head a good deal. But you mustn't be frightened. Anyone can see you've got pluck. We'll pull him through somehow, Mrs. Ferraby.'

The Cottage Hospital was aggressively cheerful with parquet floors, gay, sprawling chintzes, and vases full of painted poppy-heads. Only the heavy, varnish-like smell of chloroform betrayed it. The nurse added one more touch to the general suggestion of musical comedy, with her conscious brightness, her air of being made-up for a part. Under the hard electric light her cap and belt gleamed and glanced like mother-of-pearl, her cheeks were pink and white as the icing on a birthday cake. She smelt of some sweetish talcum powder. Joan was relieved when at last this woman left her alone with Jim. The sight of her husband had been a shock after all. She had not expected anything quite so swathed, quite so corpse-like. So corpse-like that it seemed sheer affectation for the nurse to tiptoe away like that on the points of her squeaky patent shoes. Joan sat down beside him. One hand lay outside the counterpane, bare under the thickly-bandaged arm. She touched it. It did not move, but it was warm. Someone had put a jar of chrysanthemums on the table by the bed, and their clean, earthy smell fought with the sweet, varnish fumes of the chloroform. Joan felt sick. Her head ached, and her eyes were dry and sore. She tilted the little green-shaded lamp so that it shone away from her. Its beam lit up a statuette on the mantelpiece. A vulgar little statuette. Mrs. Rennard at Weybridge had one like it. An ivory dancer with a swirl of gilded skirts. The skirts could be folded back on a hinge to show the ivory dancer standing naked. Joan remembered how very arch Mrs. Rennard was about her toy. No doubt, the nurses, too. . . . Over the dancer someone had pinned a postcard of Our Lady.

'So many nurses are Catholics,' she said to herself, fighting with her disgust.

The picture reminded her of her duty to the dy-

ing. Still keeping her right hand over Jim's, she
thrust her left into her cardigan pocket and began
to slip the small familiar beads through her fingers. Tonight she must say the fifteen decades.
Every night of her life since her First Communion
she had said her five mysteries. But the full fifteen
—those she had not said since she had prayed for
her brother Hugh at the front, kneeling, shivering
on the cold boards behind the drawn white curtains of her cubicle. How kind they had all been
at school when the news of Hugh's death had
come. How many holy pictures had been thrust
into her prayer-book: 'To darling Joan, with
much love and deepest sympathy.' 'To dear little
Joan, from her friend Muriel E. de M. *Rien ne nous
rend si grands qu'une grande douleur.*' 'To Joany, on
the saddest day of her life. I will pray for him.'

She chased away the distractions, and brought
her mind back with a jerk to Jim and the Finding
of Our Lord in the Temple. Yet she had never
been distracted when she prayed for Hugh. Every
Our Father, every Hail Mary, had been as
rounded, as deep, as perfect as she could make it.

It was difficult to pray for the ordinary Jim,
whose principal passions were his golf handicap,
and his racing cars. She must concentrate on the
figure on the bed. That bandaged thing was impersonal. It was no longer her husband. It was

simply a type of human suffering, and, as such, she could fit it into a niche in her mind. She managed four decades with perfect recollection. Then she slipped again. She found herself at a large bead when she thought she was in the middle of a Mystery. Hugh kept coming back into her mind. The wound of twelve years ago had begun to throb and ache. In vain she kept saying to herself: 'My husband—Jim—is lying there dying. We have been married eleven years. We love each other.' With the hammer strokes of a nervous headache, each one falling faster, heavier, more precisely, an old, agonized cry beat in her brain, 'If only I could have sat by Hugh like this.' For Hugh had died of wounds in a German Field Hospital, and she did not know whether he had even asked for her.

She gave up trying to say her rosary and studied the figure in the bed. Why could she not feel more? Was she stunned? Would it hurt later on? When she had heard of Hugh's death the pain had been fierce and quick, like a burn. For days it had gone on like that, blistering, scorching. When it died down at last, something had died in her. There was a patch in her mind that was burnt, dried up, where nothing would grow again. Hadn't she loved Jim? Of course she had. He had been so kind all that dreadful

year after Hugh's death. He had given her the
small son whom Joan still called Bingo because
she could not bring herself to use his name of
Hugh. Perhaps she and Jim hadn't very much in
common. It was an axiom in her family that he
wasn't 'good enough' for her. But she was grateful for him. Yes—loved him. He was her husband.

She looked at him and noticed again how long
and thin his body was under the sheets. She remembered noticing that on the first night of their
honeymoon when she had lain awake nearly all
the night in the stuffy Paris bedroom listening to
the unfamiliar treble and bass of the horses' bells
and the carts over the cobbles. His hand lying
under her own looked queerly helpless and exposed. She looked at it very carefully, noticing
the spring of the fingers, the flatness of the nails,
the broad spatula of the thumb. The hand had a
white, exhausted look that was pathetically unlike
Jim. There was a little scar that she did not remember.

'I don't suppose I've ever noticed his hands before,' she admitted. For the first time in eleven
years, she was looking at her husband with curiosity. She wished she could see his face. Perhaps
if she could see him now, unconscious that she
was watching him, something would be revealed

to her, something she had missed in him, missed in her marriage.

Jim had never understood her. They both took that for granted. For the first time it occurred to her that she might not have understood him. His queer passion for speed. It meant something to him, merely moving quickly from place to place. She had laughed at him so often for it. Oh! quite kindly. As you laugh at a child. She remembered him standing only the other day by the Renault. Enormous and shrouded, the big car had looked like a hearse in the small garage.

'I'd like to go on till I'm burnt up,' he had said in a funny apologetic voice, 'Breakfast in Liver-pool—Lunch in Aberdeen——' The words had trailed away into a laugh under her look.

Last year they had flown to Paris. Jim had been as rapt as a schoolboy on his first motor-bike.

'Watch the wheels jump off the ground,' he had shouted to her above the shattering roar of the engine.

Up in the air, he kept passing her little notes with the speed of the plane written on them. She smiled at them, bored but resolutely amiable, and consoled herself with looking down at the fields and houses below. The neatness of it all en-chanted her; the tiny lakes, the miniature houses, the tombstones no bigger than lozenges. It was

like a toy farm Hugh had given her. How she
had hated it when the aeroplane swerved and
tilted, when the ground began to rush up to them
at a sickening angle. And then she had seen
Jim's face with his mouth open and his face in a
sort of rapture. She had had to laugh although
she was angry and frightened. She had described
it to her bridge four afterwards as 'almost a
religious look'.

Religion. He had been so kind to her. Of
course he had never understood her religion,
never understood the sense it gave her of power,
of swiftness, of lightness. In the midst of a dull
party she would be conscious of wings folded inside her. That was it. That was her exquisite
secret. She was able to fly. How did Jim live
without some private flame? Perhaps he, too,
had his secret, perhaps, after this, they could find
a radiance they could both share. But was 'after
this' possible?

She fancied the hand on the sheet was growing
colder. Perhaps that was the best thing for them
both. The nurse had hinted at horrors. In spite
of that professional brightness, the woman hadn't
been able to help gloating a little. And it had
been Jim's fault. That was what she couldn't
make out. He was such a marvellous driver. She
could hear Mrs. Rennard trilling, 'Why, Mrs.

Ferraby, your husband drives like the angel Gabriel.'

What was that the nurse had said? 'You'd almost have thought he *wanted* to smash himself up, poor fellow.'

Something seemed to dissolve inside her. She felt weak and frightened. 'Jim—oh, Jim,' she whispered. In a moment she was on her knees beside him, kissing his limp, heavy hand as she had never kissed his mouth. 'I do understand—I do.'

There were tears on her lashes; slow, hot, difficult tears, as if her eyes were bleeding.

She did not hear the door open. The matron had to touch her shoulder before she would look up.

'Mrs. Ferraby, I'm afraid we've made rather a dreadful mistake,' she said. 'I was out when you came, and one of the junior nurses brought you here. She mixed up two cases. Your husband is in another room.' Still holding the stranger's hand, Joan Ferraby looked up wildly. 'Then take me to him, quickly. Has he asked for me?'

'My dear, he asked for no one.'

'You mean?'

'I'm afraid so. Just after you arrived. He passed away without any pain. Unconscious. He would not have known you.'

Far away she felt the matron's arm fall across her shoulder.

Mechanically she groped for her dropped rosary and stumbled to her feet. So he had eluded her after all.

The Rich Woman

THE first time I saw Belle Chandler was a few weeks before my marriage to her husband's nephew, Harry Grayle.

I had heard a certain amount about Belle before I met her. Harry's youngest uncle Conway Chandler (he was only thirty at the time of our wedding) was her third and richest husband. No one knew her exact age. Harry's mother said to me once, 'Belle certainly doesn't look her years, whatever they are. And she's one of those women who have an uncanny power over men. If anything happened to Con, I've no doubt she could replace him.'

I asked what had happened to Mrs. Chandler's first two husbands.

'One's still alive. He must be quite an old man now. The other died, but she didn't wait to be a widow. She left the first for the second, and the second for Con. Belle seems to get a new lease of life with each divorce. The fact remains, she's too old to give Con an heir. I fancy it shakes her a little. The last time I saw them together I had the notion she was riding him on a shade too tight a rein.'

When I showed the note, in large, decorative,

slightly back-handed writing, inviting me to come down to Malisfont with Haıry, Lady Grayle's forehead puckered.

'I wonder what Belle's after,' she said. 'If I didn't know that Harry bores her, I'd say, "Laura, my dear, look out." '

'Even though he's her nephew by marriage?'

'She likes to keep in practice. You may even have to look out for yourself. She can't bear to leave anything just as she finds it, whether it's a house or a human being.'

Then she added, in the public voice the family used when they mentioned her, 'You'll be charmed with her, of course—she's a most fascinating woman.'

'Malisfont's a queer house,' Harry said, as the car slithered slowly between the tall hedges of the drive. 'I don't mean haunted. Belle wouldn't stand for ghosts. She can't bear anything gloomy.'

'This drive's gloomy enough,' I pointed out. 'So were those sham Gothic lodges. She might at least have taken the gratings off the windows.'

Harry smiled. 'Wait till you see the dungeons —genuine Victorian dungeons. Belle grows orchids in 'em. Malisfont is a "folly", really. The old boy who built it couldn't bear people to see him. There's a mile and a half of cloisters in this park; put up so that he could take exercise without being spied on. Everyone said Belle was crazy herself to make Uncle Con buy the place. But she adores it. She's been here over two years. Must be a record for her.'

'Your mother said she was always moving.'

'It's a mania with her. She buys houses, guts them, completely redoes them. Then, as soon as she's made a place absolutely marvellous, she gets sick of it and wants a new one. Her other husbands hadn't long enough purses to stand the strain. Luckily Con has.'

'Doesn't he get restive?'

'No. He's just as bad in his own way. Can't stick to anything long. Mamma says he's become a millionaire out of sheer boredom. He can't stop inventing. He's been inventing new types of engine ever since he was eighteen. Car, yacht, plane—it's all one to him. And they're all winners!'

'What's he like?'

'Good-looking chap. All the Mr. Belles have been that. Otherwise . . . well . . . if you didn't know he was a genius, you might think his mind had stopped somewhere around thirteen. Mad on every new game and gadget that comes out. Can't be still a moment. Mealtimes are agony to him. He bolts his food like a schoolboy, so he's always finished first. Then he'll fish something out of his pocket and start jiggering with it. A Chinese puzzle or a bit of string to tie knots in. He liked me when I was a kid . . . it's a sin Belle can't produce some for him . . . but men bore him unless they're mechanics or speed-racing johnnies.'

'What about women?'

'Oh, he likes *them* all right. Or did. "Many and often" was his motto before he married. But Belle's got him hypnotized. He never even glances aside—though she's old enough to be his mother.'

'Doesn't want to, or daren't?'

'Genuinely doesn't want to, it seems. There are rumours they have rows, of course. But no one's ever caught them at it.'

It was not only because I was impatient to see the Chandlers that the drive seemed interminable. Harry had slowed the car down till we were scarcely moving.

'I didn't know you *could* drive so slowly.'

He said with unexpected fierceness:

'I'd drive fast enough if we were going away from this rotten house.'

'Harry, what *is* wrong with Malisfont?'

He speeded up a little and answered without looking at me:

'Goodness knows. Nothing probably. Certainly nothing to do with the old maniac and his dungeons and cloisters. Anyway, inside it's as cheerful as can be. Almost too cheerful if you ask me. That's Belle again. She's a Christian Scientist, you know. Says ugliness comes from evil thoughts and so on.'

'She doesn't feel the old maniac left the wrong kind of atmosphere?'

'That's the funny thing. Usually she simply tears a house to pieces before she'll live in it. But except for paint and so on, she hasn't altered Malisfont. Yet it's certainly *her* house now. I can't imagine anyone daring to live there after her.'

He was silent for a moment. Then suddenly he turned a puzzled face to me.

'You know, Laura, Malisfont's all right and Belle's all right. But I'm damned if I like the two of them together.'

We slid round a bend. The hedges on either side came to an abrupt full stop with a pillar, and there was the great house with its towers and terraces and its sweep of lawn dotted with cedars. Two projecting arms of the cloisters enclosed it like the walls of a medieval city, reflecting their red bricks and grey flints in a moat as still as a misted looking-glass. It was at once impressive and grotesque: a red-and-grey neo-Gothic castle with crenellated battlements and cross-bow windows in its turrets. The iron-studded door in the porch was open, and in the doorway stood Belle Chandler.

I saw a tall woman: full, supple, and erect, wearing a knitted dress with a fur scarf flung over her shoulders. She bent her head down, smiling, more as if to expose her face to me than to study mine. I saw a wide mouth with carved edges like an Egyptian statue's, hazel eyes slanting up to the temples, a turned-up nose with sensual nostrils, and dark-brown hair with a single streak of white. Her make-up was subdued but deliberate; the artifice seemed as natural to her skin as the bloom on an apricot. But I cannot describe Belle with my eyes only. She affected all my senses. I was simultaneously aware of her rose-geranium scent, a peculiar hum in her voice like that of a stringed instrument, and the firm, elastic texture of her flesh. When she kissed me, I had the shivering sensation in the roof of my mouth I always have when an animal licks me.

She held my arm close against her side as we passed into the great hall. The stained-glass windows and vaulted roof gave it the air of a church turned to secular uses. There was even an organ loft at one end. At the other was a low dais on which stood an open grand piano massed round with pots of hydrangeas. Chairs and sofas covered with gay chintz were scattered about; beautiful rugs made islands on the stone floor; the silver on the tea-table winked in the glow of a huge log fire in front of which a Clumber was dozing. Yet, in spite of all this opulent brightness, the effect was disquieting.

I remembered Harry's 'Almost too cheerful', and was seized with a sudden need to exchange a word or a look with him. If I had dared, I would have slipped my arm out of Belle's, but that soft pressure was inexorable. I could only turn my head in his direction. He was but a few steps behind us, yet I had the impression that he was as remote as the friend on the quay when one's ship puts out from land.

'Come and take your things off,' said Belle. 'I hope—yes, I believe—you'll like the room I've chosen for you.'

I remember nothing she said as, linked close, we walked along white-walled passages and climbed broad, shallow stairs. I remember the feel of her body, heavy yet lithe, and how I instinctively adapted my movements to hers, as if we were dancing together. I remember, too, how her low-pitched voice with its humming overtone seemed to invest the usual hostess chatter with some private meaning. She drawled a little, as if she caressed each word before she let it go. When she spoke, her wide, finely-cut lips hardly changed their contours, but her brows and eyelids were all the time in play. The short, thick lashes fluttered like wings, and deep creases came and went at the corners of her eyes. In most women the lower part of the face decays first, but there were no lines round Belle's mouth, and the chin and the full, round neck were as firm as a statue's. Only about the eyes had the skin lost its resilience and parched into fine wrinkles.

She drew my attention to this or that detail of the house, and I said mechanically, 'Yes . . . wonderful', or 'I love that'. I was too conscious of her presence to have more than a vague impression of space and whiteness, of garlanded cornices, blue Ming vases, and tubs of flowering plants. The only thing of which I was acutely aware was the smell of the house: a compound of peat, wood-smoke, rose-geranium, and the faintest possible hint of mould.

All this time, beyond a careless greeting at the door, Belle had taken no notice of Harry. He hung always a little behind us as we strolled and paused. When at last we reached the door of my room, she said over her shoulder:

'You've got your usual room, Harry. Go down

to the hall when you're ready. Con's probably in by now.'

It was a beautiful room into which she drew me, shutting the door behind us with a definite air of exclusion. I half-expected that she was going to kiss me again. Instead she disengaged her arm and moved away, saying:

'Rather a nice view, isn't it?'

'Yes, lovely,' I felt suddenly lost and foolish.

The three tall windows with their *toile de Jouy* curtains looked over the terrace, moat, and park to wooded hills.

'I quite enjoyed furnishing it. Yet I'm not absolutely satisfied. Take a good look and tell me what you think. You've got a fresh eye.'

There were presses and chests of silvery-brown wood, carved with fruit and flowers, and a mirror supported by dolphins. The bed, too, was carved in elegant swags touched here and there with faded gilt. The old silk rugs seemed to glow and change colour in their own inner light. The walls were a very pale grey, and the only modern things in the room, vast, plump armchairs covered in a rather unusual grey chintz with a scribbled yellow pattern, fitted surprisingly well into their setting. There was nothing to recall Malisfont's odd façade but the mock Gothic windows and the stone fireplace in which logs were burning.

I thought the room beautiful, and said so. As if she had not heard or were no longer interested, Belle drawled:

'The logs are mainly for show. I always have central heating as well. I loathe cold, don't you? And discomfort of any kind.'

I had never seen such luxury before and wanted to say so. But I was struck with such shyness that I might have been twelve instead of nineteen.

'Perhaps it's the chintz,' she said suddenly. 'I had it made to my own design. But they took such ages over it. By the time the stuff arrived, I'd lost interest.'

Finding nothing to say, I nodded, with what I hoped was a sophisticated smile, and spread out my fingers to the fire. Belle swooped towards me and seized both my hands.

'What a bitter little smile, Laura. One would think you were disillusioned already. And you're only at the beginning. Life should be so wonderful for you of all people.'

I looked into her eyes, changeable eyes of no definable colour, diminished by age, yet brilliant between the short, dark lashes.

'Why for me specially?' Shyness made my voice sound like a pert schoolgirl's.

She smiled.

'You're sensitive. You want the finest and best

as I do. You haven't quite come to life yet, Laura, have you? You'll be lovely, darling, when you're really happy.'

Without meaning to, I blurted out:

'Never, never as lovely as you,' and felt myself turn scarlet.

Belle gave a contented laugh and patted my cheek with a touch light as a kitten's paw.

'I know how to make myself happy,' she said. 'I'll teach you if you'll let me.'

She slipped my coat from my shoulders, and I stood there very conscious of my cheap ready-made suit.

'That green is good with your eyes,' she said kindly. 'How I should adore to design clothes for you. Of course you've got most of your trousseau by now?'

'What there is of it,' I said, feeling suddenly enough at ease to smile at her.

She clasped her hands in front of her like a pleading child.

'Let's go shopping together. Yes, darling, *please*. It would be such a treat for me. It's such fun having a pretty young thing to dress.'

'It's angelic of you, Mrs. Conway. But really, I don't . . .'

'Not Mrs. Conway,' she interrupted. 'I want you to call me by my real name.'

'But really, Belle . . .' I could get no farther.

She laughed and slipped her arm under mine again.

'That's settled. I usually get what I want, you know. That's because I always want lovely things. I suppose we'd better go back to those men. What a bore! I shouldn't say that to you, should I? Are you madly, madly in love? Or don't you know yet? Poor Harry. Anyone can see you've bewitched him.'

She drew my arm against her side and laughed again.

'I never thought Harry and I would have anything in common,' she said.

As we drew near the great hall I was puzzled by a strange noise, the heavy, irregular hammering of wood on stone.

'Con and his latest toy,' Belle said. 'Infants, aren't they?'

Harry was standing by the fire with his hands in his pockets, tickling the fat Clumber with his foot. He had an abandoned look. The other man in the hall took no notice of us. His handsome, dark face was set in a scowl of concentration as he hopped about the stone floor on a pogo stick.

We spent four days at Malisfont. Often, for hours at a time, I did not see Belle. But I was

conscious of her at every moment, most of all
when I was alone with Harry. Each time we met
again, she gave me a peculiar look and smile as if
our intimacy had grown in absence. Once she
took me into her bedroom, which was full of
white fur rugs and old gilt furniture, and opened
cupboard after cupboard of clothes. It had never
occurred to me that a woman could possess so
many. There were shelves heaped with chiffon
and satin underclothes, folded as carefully as in a
shop; each neat pile covered with a square of
handmade lace. There were rows of apparently
unworn shoes from brogues that shone like chest-
nuts to virgin white buckskins and jewelled san-
dals. One wardrobe was entirely filled with furs:
sable, ermine, mink, and chinchilla. She made
me try on fur coats, parading in them like a man-
nequin while she watched me with narrowed,
critical eyes. There was one, a soft squirrel cloak,
dyed a tawny gold, which she said was too short
for her and the wrong colour but 'might have
been made' for me. The furs, like all her posses-
sions, smelt of rose-geranium. Then, suddenly
tiring of them, she threw the coats in a heap and
produced a great velvet-lined jewel-case. It was
like an Arabian Nights casket: pearls, diamonds,
emeralds, sapphires lay in a glittering tangle. She
plunged her short, white fingers into the heap,

pulling out now an emerald bracelet, now a string of diamonds.

'I love jewels,' she said. 'But only to look at and play with. I never wear any of these things now.' All the time I knew Belle, I never saw her with anything but the double row of pearls she wore night and day and one square emerald that almost hid her three wedding-rings.

She screwed up her eyes at me. 'You ought never to wear anything but pearls, Laura. I can't bear fair women in anything that glitters. Harry should have had more sense than to give you a diamond ring.'

She disentangled a string of pearls and clasped it round my neck. Its light weight against the warmth of my skin was cold as something fresh from the sea. Belle must have seen from my eyes how much I wanted it.

She considered the effect with her head on one side. 'Perfect. Pearls go dull on some women, but they won't on you. You've got affinity with them, like me. It's as if your skin were waiting for them to bring it to life.'

I was about to unclasp them, but she stopped me.

'Leave them for the moment. I like to see you in them.'

Then she began to tell me how she had

acquired every piece of furniture in the room. I tried to listen attentively, but I could think of nothing but the pearls. I fancied I could feel them growing warm against my neck. She took me into her bathroom, and I patiently admired every detail, the sunk bath with silver taps shaped like mermaids; the Venetian mirror, wreathed in tinted-glass flowers, the green mosaic floor, even the eighteenth-century porcelain door-knob.

The gong sounded for luncheon. She put her arm through mine, and we walked back through the bedroom. At the door she stopped suddenly:

'Oh, I forgot, darling. My pearls.'

I unclasped them clumsily. I could hardly bear to let them go. She watched me with bright, narrowed eyes. As I put them in her hand, she held them for a moment against her cheek.

'Warm from your skin,' she said smiling. 'Even in this short time you have revived them. You must wear them for me again.'

She went back to her dressing-table, took out the jewel box which she had locked, and dropped them in carelessly.

'A pretty little string, isn't it? I was very fond of it till Con gave me these. It's bad for pearls never to be worn.'

Her carved lips had their sweetest smile as she locked the box.

The night before we left, she came into my bedroom while I was brushing my hair in front of the fire. In honour of Malisfont, I was wearing the dressing-gown I had made for my trousseau and which I had not meant to wear till my wedding-night. It was of peach-coloured satin, trimmed with swansdown, wildly unpractical for the sort of life Harry and I would be leading (we were just fledged from an acting school, and hoping to get parts on tour), but, after years of school flannel and ripple-cloth, I had a craving for silly, pretty things. And when Belle, after the softest of taps, walked in in a wonderful négligée of white velvet and fur, I was glad I was wearing it.

She took the brush from my hands saying, 'Let me do that,' and began to brush in long, caressing strokes.

'I've wanted to do this ever since I saw you,' she said. 'Promise me you'll never cut your hair. You'll ruin your appearance. It will get darker, too. You'll lose this wonderful silvery fairness.'

She brushed on rhythmically, talking in a soft, purring voice, till I felt half-hypnotized. Suddenly she said:

'You'll come to Malisfont for your honeymoon, won't you?'

I started out of my trance, breaking the rhythm of a brush stroke and murmured something.

'I've spoken to Harry,' she said. 'He's perfectly willing if you are. Of course Con and I will go away and leave you the place to yourselves.'

I think I tried to protest, but she merely kissed me and said:

'That's settled, darling. You have made me so happy. I love brides, and so does Malisfont.'

She put her hand under my chin and looked into my eyes.

'You are a Roman Catholic, aren't you, Laura? I suppose your church is very strict about . . . well, before marriage and so on?'

'Yes.'

'All the better,' she said with a smile. 'It makes love so much more wonderful. I am a Scientist: did you know?'

I nodded.

'It's all the same thing. We worship the same Spirit. The Spirit of joy and beauty. Ugliness and sorrow are the only sins. We must never let our thoughts be contaminated by contact with error. For that is what ugliness and suffering and depression are. Even Con is in error sometimes you know. But if our thoughts are happy and beautiful, we shall be happy and beautiful too, and *everything* we do will be right.'

She had a serious, exalted look. I felt uneasy

yet I could not bring myself to contradict or interrupt.

'Sweet Laura,' she said. 'Nothing gloomy must
ever touch your life. In my philosophy, goodness
and beauty are the same.'

I laughed.

'You must be very, very good, Belle.'

She smiled, but still with that air of lofty
earnestness.

'We are what we make ourselves, Laura.'

Then her expression changed. Her eyes
crinkled at the corners: she was all warmth and
pleading, as if for a moment uncertain of her
charm.

'I want to ask you a great favour, Laura.'

I was in her power again, and would have said
'Yes' to anything.

'I want you to promise that your first child
shall be born here.'

I promised, feeling extraordinarily unreal as I
did so. Or was it that my own life apart from
Malisfont had become unreal? I felt dizzy and
suddenly very tired, as if all the life had gone out
of me. Belle stood up. Her face was transfigured:
it seemed to have become at the same time much
older and ageless. Some power seemed to inform
her whole body; the white dressing-gown might
have been a priestess's robe. For the first time, I

felt frightened of her. I wanted to revoke my promise; to say that I never wanted to come to Malisfont again. But I was too helpless to speak. She moved very softly over to the door, said, almost aloofly, 'Good-night, dear. And thank you,' and was gone before I could force my lips open.

I slept badly that night, oppressed with dreams. It was one of those nights when one seems to dream with one's eyes open and wakes from one nightmare into another. So, to this day, I do not know whether or not I had a hallucination. But, at one point, as I was lying there, awake as I believe, I felt a weight on my bed and opened my eyes. The room, in the light of the dying log-fire, was perfectly recognizable; my dressing-gown hung over the chair just as I had thrown it off, the dolphin-supported mirror was tilted at the angle I had left it. But, sitting on my bed, in the furry white négligée, looking intently at me and smiling, was Belle Chandler. It seemed to me that, without a word on either side, I returned that look until my eyelids grew so heavy that I had to close them. When I opened them again, the room was empty.

The next time I saw Malisfont was on my honeymoon. Belle did not come to our wedding, though I saw her once or twice in London during the interval. Harry was right. Away from Malis-

font she was oddly diminished; she seemed little
more than an elderly, still handsome woman in a
mink coat. She took me shopping as she had
promised. We spent hours in expensive little
places where she made me try on endless hats or
asked the mannequins to parade whole series of
dresses. She would order things and then coun-
termand them, whispering to me that she was not
quite satisfied and we must try elsewhere. In the
end she bought me nothing but a veil and a
wreath of orange blossom, far more expensive,
but no prettier, than the one I had bought already, and an exquisite little scarlet leather bag
which did not go with anything I possessed.

When Lady Grayle heard of these expeditions
she smiled ambiguously.

'Belle has certainly taken you up, my dear.
Make hay while the sun shines. If she asks you
what you want for a wedding-present, don't ask
for anything niggling. And for goodness' sake,
don't leave it to her.'

I did not admit that this was just what I had
done. Nor that Belle, with her sweetest, most
enigmatic smile had answered, 'I think it will be
something you'll like very much.'

She had decided not to come to the wedding
on the plea of getting everything ready for us at
Malisfont, but she had insisted that the flowers I

was to carry should come from her hot-houses.
When I told Harry this, something in his face
made me wish I had refused.

'Damn it,' he said, 'Belle's running us a bit too
much for my fancy. She might at least have left
those to me. Still, I can't compete with the Malisfont orchids.'

The flowers did not arrive till the very last moment. Indeed, I had already left for the church
and the Conway's chauffeur had to pursue us. As
I was waiting in a side-chapel, he thrust a bouquet
of slightly crushed lilies into my hands and a blue
leather jewel-case. The case was not new, and my
hopes rose. I snapped it open. A note from Belle
lay above some object wrapped in silk tissue.

'All my love, darling little Laura. Wear these
today for my sake. To me, ivory is *you*. I am so
terribly sorry about your lilies. I gathered them
and tied them up myself, but my naughty old
spaniel worried them, and there was no time to
pick more. But all my thoughts for you are in
them.'

The necklace was a perfectly new one of ivory
beads such as all the shops were full of that year.
They lay in my hand cold and dead-looking as
bone.

'Don't wear them,' my bridesmaid whispered,
'she's not here; she'll never know.'

But, perhaps from cowardice for I hated them
at sight, I did wear them, and all through the ceremony I was conscious of their chilly weight on
my neck.

As Harry and I drove down to Malisfont, I
think the same thought occurred to both of us.
Once or twice when the car slowed down, we exchanged looks as if to say, 'Shall we cut and run?'
We half-expected to find that no preparations had
been made for us. But we were wrong. The
house was full of flowers, and the room where I
had slept before was wonderfully decorated with
white camellias and the famous Malisfont orchids.
When we came down to dinner we found a small
candle-lit table drawn up by a fire laid with
Belle's most exquisite glass and silver. There was
a touch of fairy-tale extravagance about the whole
thing. We were so obviously awaited, so un-
obtrusively served, so emphatically left to ourselves that we became self-conscious as we had
never been before and found ourselves talking
with a false brightness, as if trying to impress a
stranger.

At one point, Harry suddenly said:

'Laura, there's something wrong about all this.
I feel as if we were acting. Someone's *producing*
us. Don't you feel we're speaking lines?'

I tried to say with conviction that probably

everyone felt the same on the first night of a honey-moon. But the conviction was not there.

This sense of dreamy unreality did not leave us the next day or the next. The huge empty house, the park, the formal gardens, began to oppress us. We felt like prisoners. On the third day, after breakfast, Harry said: 'Let's take one of the cars and get away by ourselves.' Neither of us had heard the butler come in—he moved always as quietly as a cat—and it gave us a shock to hear him say:

'I'm so sorry, sir. Mr. and Mrs. Chandler have taken the Hudson, and the Rolls is away being overhauled. There is nothing in the garage but the station van.'

'Then we'll take that,' said Harry impatiently.

'I'm *very* sorry, sir,' said the urbane voice. 'It is in use this morning.'

Harry swore, tugged open the French window and strode out on to the terrace. I would have followed, but something restrained me. Perhaps it was the butler's eye. I was desperately anxious to behave as if I had been married a very long time.

I got up and walked through the door he held open for me. I intended to make my way through the house, go out by the front porch, and join Harry outside. But, as I stepped out into the long, white passage, I heard something which made my heart miss a beat. Someone was playing the piano in the great hall.

The sound compelled me to follow it to its source. I had no doubt who was playing, but I had to see for myself.

She was sitting sideways to me at the piano on the dais. She was dressed in travelling-clothes with a little fur toque and a veil. I stood for what seemed several minutes watching her absorbed profile. She was playing idly, without music, staring straight in front of her. At last she turned her head and sent me a smile. Her left hand continued to make chords and arpeggios as she beckoned me with her right.

Her look, as I came closer, was sly and pleading.

'I'm not here, really,' she said. 'Take no notice of me.'

She gave her explanation while her hands continued to move mechanically over the keyboard. She and Con had dashed back—literally for an hour. They were going to Brooklands for some speed-trials. Con wasn't perfectly satisfied with the tuning-up of his car. I knew what Con was, didn't I? There was some bit of fidgeting with the engine he was doing at that moment in the garage. I said it was absurd, if they were as near as Brooklands, not to sleep in their own house.

'And interrupt the lovebirds? *Never*, darling. Malisfont is *your* house this week. And, in any case, Con and I are going north straight from the meeting.'

I began to thank her, clumsily, for all she had done for us. She smiled, kindly yet a little impatiently, like someone hearing a story they know already.

Suddenly she lifted her hands from the keyboard and opened her arms to me. I felt once again the warmth of the lithe, heavy body; smelt her familiar perfume; was aware of that shivering sensation on my palate.

'Ah, Laura, Laura. Is it all being wonderful . . . as wonderful as you dreamed?'

I murmured something, I don't know what. But, in that moment, I was convinced that she knew as well as I did that it was not being wonderful at all. I was convinced too (though I never had any evidence of this) that she had been at Malisfont all the time.

However, she really did go that day. She summoned Harry and me to watch her drive off with Con. The chauffeur was to follow with the racing car, and Con lingered a little, giving him last-minute instructions.

143

Suddenly, he hesitated.

'I'll drive her myself, Parry. You take Mrs. Chandler.'

Belle swerved round in her seat. Her face, in the April sunlight, looked suddenly old and mask-like. But her voice was sweet, as she said:

'No, darling. *You're* driving me.'

'*All* right, Belle,' he said sullenly. When I had stayed at Malisfont before, Conway Chandler had taken practically no notice of me. But, now, he suddenly stepped up to me and said:

'I haven't kissed the bride. Uncle's privilege, eh, Laura?'

'Con, are we *never* going to get off?' Belle's voice was like the swish of a lash.

He started, but he kissed me all the same. I caught the look he exchanged with Harry before he jumped into the driving-seat, and it was not one I wish to see again. The car shot forward with a jerk and was swallowed up between the dark hedges of the drive. Probably our rather half-hearted 'good-bye' and 'good luck' were drowned by the roar of the engine, for neither of them turned a head.

Harry said, 'I wouldn't be surprised if he killed her one of these days.'

But it was Con who was killed, that very afternoon, at Brooklands. We did not hear the news for a day or two. An hour after we saw them off, we were on our way to London, and, before the evening papers came out, we were heading for Cornwall in Harry's old car.

If we thought that, by leaving Malisfont, we could throw off whatever blight had fallen on us, we were wrong. The village people watched us with friendly irony as we walked up every morning from the sea with arms entwined. But every night, like actors during an interval, we returned to our separate selves.

The summer that followed our wedding was unusually hot. The little house, that had seemed so charming when we took it, became like a stifling box as one airless day followed another. It was so hot that the water ran warm in the taps and candles bent in their sockets. I was tired and languid in a way that I had never been in my life; it seemed to me I had grown ten years older. I became too apathetic to go round the agents looking for a part, and left Harry to go by himself. Often I would sit the whole day in the tiny house we had taken, leaving meals uncleared for hours. Some days I felt too weary even to dress properly, but sat about in a dressing-gown with my hair loose and unbrushed.

Harry was first worried, then irritated by the change in me. I had no explanation to offer; I knew that physically there was nothing the matter with me. After a time he took to leaving me alone for longer and longer intervals, on the excuse that he must meet as many people as possible, if he was ever to get a part. Sometimes I made a scene, nagging him feebly long after I had gained my point, simply because I could not summon up enough energy to stop.

When Belle's note inviting me to Malisfont came, I felt too indifferent to go. But Harry unexpectedly insisted.

'I've come to the conclusion I loathe Belle,' he said. 'But you ought to go. It'll be cooler down there. The change may do you good. God knows you need something to pull you out of this.'

The lawns at Malisfont were parched and cracked; the grass was bleached; the moat had shrunk and looked stagnant. Leaves had begun to shrivel like paper and were falling already, though it was only July. Belle looked at me searchingly when I arrived, stroked my hair and said I was pale. Her manner was kind, but absent: once or twice I caught her looking at me as if she were puzzled or displeased about something.

The first night, we dined alone in the small room where Harry and I had had our wedding-supper. The French windows were open, for the

sake of coolness, and Belle sat with her back to
them. She was all in black, with a length of white
tulle twisted carelessly round her thick, creamy
neck and half-covering the pearls that hung in the
deep opening of her dress. I told her she looked
like a portrait, sitting there against the background of balustrade and yew-hedge and darken-
ing sky. She smiled faintly in the way I remembered so well, hardly moving the outlines of her
Egyptian mouth. Then she suddenly narrowed
her eyes at me.

'It that your *only* evening-frock, darling?'

I felt myself flush.

'Well . . . my only decent one. You said you
liked it.'

It was a pink dress I had bought for my trousseau; the most expensive dress I had ever had in
my life. I had worn it the first time I had stayed at
Malisfont, and Belle had said, 'You look charming
—as if you were wearing a great rose upside
down.'

'Did I? I don't remember. Anyhow I'd forgotten it was such a *vivid* pink. Or is it just because you're so pale?'

I was anything but pale at that moment. I felt
the blood rushing up over my face and neck till
the skin seemed as if it would burst.

'You've got fatter, haven't you, darling?' she

went on. 'I suppose people take it as a sign that married life suits you.'

I could not help it. My eyes suddenly filled with idiotic tears.

Suddenly she put her arm across the table and took my hand.

'How sensitive you are, Laura,' she said very softly. 'I suppose it's the baby, isn't it? You must be very, very careful to have right thoughts.'

'Baby?' I blurted out. 'Did you think I was going to have a baby?'

'Well . . . aren't you?'

'No.'

'Are you *quite* sure?'

'Yes, positive.'

She took her hand away and said coldly:

'Stupid of me.'

After dinner, we went into the great hall. Belle hardly spoke to me. She sat down at the piano and played absently. Suddenly she got up in the middle of a phrase and left me alone for a long time: I fancied I could hear the disconnected murmur of her voice, behind a door that opened off the hall. When, at last, she returned, she turned a bright, false hostess's smile on me.

'Monstrous of me to desert you so long, darling. I hope you haven't been bored to tears. I had to make some tiresome 'phone calls.'

She sat down again, making desultory conversation, asking me questions and not listening to the answers. Soon she yawned quite frankly.

'Absurd how sleepy this weather makes one. What do you say to bed? You look absolutely worn out.'

I got up, but she remained in her chair.

'That's right. You run along. I'll stay up a little. I like to think at this time of night. I suppose Roman Catholics call it "meditating".'

I stooped to kiss her, but, with the faintest movement, she averted her cheek.

'Too hot even for kissing,' she said. 'Don't you agree?'

As I walked away, feeling painfully clumsy in the pink dress I had already begun to loathe, she called after me:

'Oh, Laura. Something I meant to tell you. Would you think me a perfect monster if I turned you out of your room tomorrow night?'

I stopped and looked back at her.

'No, of course not.'

'That 'phone call. It was two friends of mine who are getting married tomorrow. Something's gone wrong with their plans. They wanted to know if they could come here for their honeymoon. I hadn't the heart to say "No". And the room you're in is really the only *possible* one for a married couple.'

'Of course, Belle. I'll move my things in the morning.'

She smiled and yawned.

'Angelic of you. I knew you'd understand.'

I said awkwardly, 'Belle . . . wouldn't you rather . . . I mean, . . . wouldn't it be more tactful if I went?'

'Silly girl. Of course not. I wouldn't have you go for the world. I don't know whether you'll like Monty—it's his second marriage of course, and he's years older than she is. But you'll adore Sybil. She's ravishing. Only eighteen . . . just a slip of a girl. She looks exactly like an arum lily.'

When I saw Sybil Delahaye the next night, I had to admit that she did look like an arum lily. She was wearing her wedding-dress, which clung to her like a sheath, emphasizing her extreme slimness. Her hair was the palest ash-blonde and her skin almost as white as her dress. She might have been insipid but for a pair of brilliant blue-grey eyes with marked brows and astonishingly dark lashes.

She seemed a gentle creature, with a fawnlike shyness. I had the impression that she was afraid of her husband; a tall, heavy man with brutal good looks and a sulky voice. He kept a greedy eye on

her all through dinner, but she seldom looked at
him and I often caught her glancing at Belle, as if
for reassurance. And each time Belle answered
the look with a warm, brooding smile. Beyond
Monty Delahaye's observing how appallingly hot
it was even in the country, I do not think anyone
spoke to me all through the meal.

Very early, Belle drew Sybil away to take her
up to her room. I did not like to go out with
them, though the last thing I wanted was to be
left alone with Sybil's husband. However, after a
few minutes, he grunted, 'Think I'll finish my ci-
gar on the terrace,' and I was free. It seemed safe
to go upstairs now. Belle would be in my old
room, saying good-night to the bride, and I could
slip into my new, rather perfunctorily furnished
one unobserved.

But as I walked up the wide, shallow steps I saw
two enlaced figures, one black, one white, ahead
of me on the landing. They were apparently
studying the blue Ming vase in the niche, and
Belle was murmuring something, in her humming voice, in the girl's ear. I could not very
well retreat, but Belle must have heard me coming, for she seemed to scoop Sybil up in her bent
arm and sweep her up the next flight. At the same
time she raised her voice and I heard her say:

'Your children must be as lovely as you. You

don't know how happy you'd make me, darling, if the first one were born here.'

.   .   .   .   .

It was fifteen years before I saw Malisfont again. My marriage to Harry had long ago broken up by slow, almost imperceptible stages. When he finally came and asked me if I would divorce him, he said, with a long, puzzled look at me, 'I never imagined I'd be asking you that, Laura. What was it that went wrong with us? Or, perhaps, what was it that never went right?' But I had no answer, any more than he had. The last thing he ever said to me was, 'You know . . . I felt we never really had a fair chance.'

Belle's death I saw in the papers. She had died of cancer. An operation might have saved her, but she had refused to be treated except by a Christian Science healer. The popular dailies ran headlines about 'an Edwardian "Belle" ' and showed an old photograph of her in a Langtry bonnet and a 'last snapshot' in a cloche hat that almost hid her eyes so that I could make out little but her mouth. The coarse screen and the heavy retouching made it look like a negress's. The captions recalled her three marriages, Conway's 'tragic death' at Brooklands, and gave her age as seventy-three.

After her death, Malisfont was sold. I heard rumours that it had been used, first as a country club and then as a girls' school. Eventually it became a permanent feature among 'Desirable properties to be sold'.

One wet autumn, I found myself stranded in the little town a mile from its gates. I plucked up my courage, went to the agent and asked for the key.

'We don't give many orders to view these days,' he said. 'It's on the gloomy side at the best of times. Why don't you wait for a fine day when you can see it to advantage?' He brightened when he found I did not want him to accompany me. I managed to convince him that I already knew the house. 'It's against the rules, but I'll stretch a point,' he said, handing me a punch of rusty keys. 'You'll find the place a bit deteriorated. But Malisfont's a fine investment for someone with a bit of capital and a bit of patience. Make a first-class building site.'

A line of washing flapped forlornly in the rain at one of the lodges, but no inquisitive eyes appeared at a window.

I walked up the long drive between the dripping, unkempt laurels. At last came the bend and the abrupt full stops of the pillars, dirty grey in the wet and blotched with moss. Ahead of me stood the great, drenched, blind house, with the reflection of the cloisters dancing a little in the rain-pocked moat.

Feeling like a thief, I turned the key with difficulty in the lock of the great sham-Gothic door. I was shaking as I pushed it open. I had nerved myself to find everything different. The shock was that, after fifteen years, it was all perfectly recognizable. The chapel-like hall, now completely bare, had a hideous newness as if it had only just been completed. Along the passages, the white paint had turned sallow, but here and there rusty hooks stuck out from the cornice and I could remember the pictures that had hung from them.

My footsteps echoed unnaturally as I climbed the wide, shallow stairs: a faint circle was still discernible in a niche where a blue Ming vase had stood. In the passage outside the main bedrooms, I had to stand still for a moment. My heart was beating so violently that I could have sworn someone else was walking about the house. Outside her bedroom, I stopped again. I could not believe the paint on the door and on the swags above it was not fresher than the rest. Nor could I convince myself that, if I opened it, I should find the room just as it had been fifteen years ago. Up to now Malisfont had been an empty shell, but here, here I was sure I was on her track. Hardly knowing what I did, I put my lips to the panel, whispered 'Belle' and opened the door.

The room mocked me, emptier than any hitherto and mutilated. The panelling had been roughly painted a bilious fawn; rags of drugget still clung to the worn and splintered parquet. Evidently it had been used as a school dormitory; black rails and posts divided it up into skeleton cages. Yet I shut my eyes and sniffed, as if trying to catch, through all these superimposed layers of dust, varnish and stagnant air, the faintest trace of her scent. There was indeed something I could smell; mildewed and pungent, with a touch of sickening sweetness. I followed it to the door of her bathroom in the wall just left of where the great gilded dressing-table used to stand. Someone had pasted a Mabel Lucie Atwell picture of a simpering baby on one of the panels. But the old French porcelain door-knob, cracked under its greasy film of dust, was still there. I turned it and went in.

The green mosaic floor and the sunk bath were stained and dull; the silver mermaids had tarnished to a dark irridescence. But the Venetian mirror was still on the wall, so coated with dirt that my reflection swam towards me faint and discoloured as if in a muddy pool. Most of its frail glass flowers had been chipped off, but now it was surrounded by a gaudy and monstrous frame. Damp had seeped in through a crack in the outer wall; all about the mirror and nowhere else was a shapeless mass of liver and yellow fungus. I stared, disgusted and sick, almost overpowered by the corrupt, sweetish smell. And somewhere inside myself I felt, rather than heard, Harry's voice, faint but unmistakable, saying, 'I can't compete with the Malisfont orchids.'

Sed Tantum Dic Verbo

THEY say, 'Receive with dread
This strong life-giving bread
Lest you constrain the Host
To feed the carnal ghost.'

Yet how, Lord, shall I learn
Thy Body to discern?
To all Thou sayest, 'Eat,
This is the pilgrim's meat
Without which none may come
Back to his Father's home.'
Thou didst compel the least
Unto this wedding-feast;
And if, compelled, I came,
Shall I then be to blame
Because I had no dress
To clothe my nakedness?

Thou knowest I am poor.
When at the palace door
Thy servants challenged me
I had no word to say.

STRANGERS

Beckoned, then banished at Thy strange
   behest,
I learnt 'twas perilous to be Thy guest.

But in this other rite
'Tis I, I who invite,
And Thou canst not refuse
To come if I so choose.
I summon Thee at will
To vivify or kill;
For, cruel mystery,
There are two kinds in me,
So tangled in my heart
I know them not apart,
Nor which, in craving need,
I call Thee in to feed.

Lord, since I cannot swear
If I be clothed or bare,
Nor whether in this strife
I side with death or life;
If I be naked, cover
The beggar's body over
With Thine own royal cope,
And, since I dare not hope
(Even to Thy image being now quite
   blind)
Of my own wit to recognize Thy kind,

Distinguish mine and in this soul,
Where I no more unravel fair from foul,
Plunge Thy divining-rod, the two-edged
   sword.
Strike to my source; cleave, one me
   with the Word.

Surprise Visit

For over fifteen years, Julia Tye had been meaning to go back some day and look at the place, partly out of curiosity, partly to prove to herself that she could face it without a qualm. True, she did not know just where it stood, beyond that it was somewhere on London's south bank. On the morning of her release from the huge, grimed building with its dome that so deceptively suggested a church, she had been too excited to notice street names. But she remembered that, soon after leaving the iron gate in the spiked walls, the taxi had crossed a bridge over the Thames. It would have been easy enough to locate it. The place was so old and so notorious that its name had become a generic term for all institutions of its kind. It was probably featured in Baedeker. However, there was no need to consult a guidebook. All Julia had to do was to look it up in a certain classified section of the telephone directory. For some reason or other she had not done so.

This was not because she was trying to forget the period she had spent in the place all that time ago, in her early twenties. On the contrary, whenever the memory tended to fade, she deliberately recalled it. Year by year it gave her a peculiar satisfaction to measure how far and how successfully she had travelled since that deplorably bad start. Nowadays she found it more gratifying than ever. No one at Frant and Red-

wood's, that eminent publishing firm where she
held down such a highly responsible job, could
ever have suspected that 'our Miss Tye' had ever
been anything but utterly reliable. She had been a
reformed character for so long that she could
trust herself as much as her employers trusted her.
It was only when someone unexpectedly
mentioned the name of the place (though she
often mentioned it herself in the right company)
that she felt a faint, apprehensive chill.

Then, one morning, soon after her thirty-
eighth birthday, its name had leapt out at her in a
heading in a newspaper. Breaking off from the
book reviews she was studying, she switched her
eye to the paragraph in the other column. It
informed her that the place had been turned into
a War Museum. 'The Public Authorities,' she
read, 'have realised, for some considerable time,
that, judged by modern standards, the building
was unsuitable for the purpose it has served for
centuries. Since the edifice is attributed to Wren,
it was decided not to demolish it, but to use it to
house the various weapons, trophies and models
which have accumulated during two world wars.
Many of these have not hitherto been displayed
owing to lack of space. Now that certain neces-
sary internal alterations have been made, the
public will be admitted daily (public holidays
excepted) to what should prove an interesting
exhibition.'

As Julia put down the paper, she saw at once

that this was a brilliant opportunity. Now she had a really cogent reason for going back to look at the place. Seeing it from the outside would have been no real test. But to walk right into that building of her own accord, as an ordinary member of the public, free to walk out of it when she chose, would disinfect it once and for all in her imagination.

She could not go at once. Frant and Redwood were in the throes of getting out their autumn list. But even when the rush of work had slowed down, she still delayed her visit. For one thing, she was tired. Without having yet verified its exact situation, she was convinced that it was a long way away both from her home and her office and would mean a tiresome, complicated journey. For another, she had an excellent reason for not being in a hurry. Any sense of anxious compulsion would ruin the experiment. This was something to be undertaken coolly and unemotionally, at the right, the scientific moment. She was sure the analyst who had so successfully diagnosed the causes of her anti-social behaviour would agree.

There was also a third, rather odd reason why she did not yet feel quite ready to confront the place. Though she could recall a number of concrete details about the apparently endless time she had spent in it, the place itself remained unreal. She could shrink her experience into a period between two known dates, but she could not reduce the building to a concrete mass occupying a fixed point in space. Some part of her mind refused to admit that it had gone on existing independently of her, that it was solidly situated somewhere in South London. Even when she read that paragraph in the paper she had felt a faint uncertainty as if, in spite of the old notorious name, the place referred to was not *the* place. Even had there been a photograph, she would still not have been quite sure. She had never been able to rebuild it in memory as a recognisable whole.

It was months after reading the paragraph that going, as she often did in her lunch hour, to buy a ticket for a Shakespeare performance at the Old Vic, she somehow lost her way. After leaving the box-office, she walked a few blocks, absorbed in some office problem, then stopped, expecting to find herself opposite Waterloo Station. Instead, she found herself on the edge of a completely unfamiliar main road. Realising she must have taken the wrong direction, she looked back to see how far she had come from the Old Vic. It was nowhere in sight. Without realizing it, she must have turned a corner. She stood still, gazing around to try to get her bearings. And there, right opposite her, on the other side of the stream of traffic, was the place.

What startled her even more than its sudden appearance, was her instant recognition of that grimy stone facade, with steps leading up to a

pillared portico and a dome rising above. Why
was she sure that, of many London buildings of
its type, it was *the* one? Yet she had known
infallibly that it was, before she read *Imperial
War Museum* on the board at the open gate.
Could she really have registered her one remembered glimpse of its front, more than fifteen years
ago, as sharply as that? How shocked, how hurt
her father had looked, on the morning they
discharged her, when she had turned at the gate
to glance back and exclaim:

'Why, it's quite noble, when you see it from
the front! Of course, *we* never did.'

He hadn't let her linger, as she longed to, to
make out whether that slim dome, firmly
anchored above its matching stone pediment,
could possibly be the same that used to float now
here, now there, erratic as a bubble, over this or
that cliff of dingy brown brick. Even at that
moment—it came back to her now as she stared—
she had had an odd feeling that the building
corresponded with some other image, something
like a tiny snapshot printed in sepia she had seen
innumerable times. Before she could find the
connection, her father had bundled her into the
waiting taxi, and said, in a low voice, so that the
driver should not hear:

'Please God, neither you nor I will ever set
eyes on that place again. Julia, my dear, for your
own sake—as well as for mine and your mother's
—try and blot these last months out of your mind.

All we want you to do now is think ahead to a new life. The few people who know where you have been will have the decency not to mention it. So we'll make a pact here and now, shall we, never to refer to the subject again?'

In his presence, she never had referred to it. To forget was, of course, impossible, though at first she hadn't deliberately tried to recall it. It had recalled itself often enough, in the first year or two after her release, in those nightmares where she found herself back there, this time without hope of escape, being herded up and down long corridors and up steep winding stone stairs with other women or locked alone in a cell with a high, barred window, beating frantically on a blank door. But, when the nightmares became more infrequent (she hardly ever had them now) she had found it curiously fascinating to piece it all together. It was extraordinary how much she had consciously forced herself to remember, though time had had so little meaning there that it was impossible to put her memories in an orderly sequence. Long before her father's death, she had discovered there were people to whom she could talk about it quite frankly. Unconventional, broadminded people who saw nothing disgraceful about what had happened to her. With some, it even gave her a peculiar prestige. But of course there were others with whom she had to be careful; there were people who still held her father's old-fashioned views.

Sometimes it amused her, in the middle of a dull conference at Frant and Redwood's, to fancy the electrifying effect if 'our Miss Tye' suddenly announced where she had spent most of her twenty-third year.

Now, abruptly confronted with the place, she felt angry and almost insulted. It had no right to burst in on her crudely like that. She glared at it like some intrusive acquaintance who had appeared uninvited. Moreover, there was something indecent in this public exhibition of itself right on a main London road. In her imagination it had always been remote and secretive, approachable only by a maze of tortuous paths. To think it had stood there, all those years, within a few hundred yards of the Old Vic, shamelessly waiting to catch her eye!

Well, now it was there, she would call its bluff. She couldn't of course spare the time. Not that she couldn't take as long a lunch-hour as she pleased, but her desk was piled with proofs she wanted to go through herself for a final revision. It was astonishing how printers' readers, as well as authors, seemed to suffer from mental black-outs. She would go over and accost it, just as she had deliberately accosted Roberts and Patterson, all those years ago, in that night-club. She hadn't, of course, identified them so promptly, disguised in those tatty evening-frocks, with rows of coloured glass bangles wedged on their muscular arms. She had merely been aware of

two unpartnered middle-aged women, rather
pathetically out of their element, covertly staring
at her every time she stepped on to the dance-
floor. Julia was quite used to being stared at in
those days, even by women. It had seemed
rather important, as well as a pleasure, in that
first period of her 'new life' to be particularly
well-dressed and well-groomed. She had felt
unusually confident that night; looking her best,
dancing her best, enjoying being a pretty young
woman in the arms of a handsome young man. It
was he . . . which of her young men had it
been? . . . who had said irritably:

'Anyone would think those two ghastly
females knew you, the way they keep staring at
you, then putting their heads together and
whispering.'

She had laughed back:

'Oh, I've known some odd people in my time.
You'd be surprised. Next time we pass, I'll
have a good look at them.'

The moment she had recognized them over her
shoulder, she had broken away from him, in the
middle of their dance, saying:

'I certainly do know them. But I don't think
they're sure about *me.* I'm going over to speak
to them.'

'*No,* Julia,' he had said, clutching her arm.
'They're really too awful, like women policemen.'

'Perhaps that's just what they are!' she had
mocked, throwing off his arm and giving

Roberts and Patterson her most dazzling smile. 'Anyway, I'm going to have a word with them.'

'Can't it wait? This is such a marvellous tune.'

'It's an even more marvellous joke. I met them in the most *fantastic* circumstances. Perhaps I'll tell you when I get back.'

It shamed her even now to remember she couldn't have carried it off worse. She hadn't been gay and assured, or even lightly cynical. She had faltered and flushed, almost cringed, as if they were still in uniform, with bunches of keys at their belts. Pressed by the young man to tell him the marvellous joke, she had said it wasn't so very funny after all. Though the two women had left almost at once, she had been so silent and danced so badly for the rest of the evening that the young man had asked if she were ill.

Firmly, Julia crossed the road and entered the gate. Slowly and deliberately she walked up the gravel path, fixing her eyes on the building, trying to reduce it to something as impersonal as the Victoria and Albert. All at once, her knees began to tremble. Instead of the huge, three dimensional building, a tiny flat sepia replica of it danced before her retina. She blinked and it was gone again; blinked again . . . it was back, this time encircled by a scroll lettered with its old name, as she had seen it day after day on .mugs and plates. She knew at last why she had recognised the place at sight. It ought to have reassured her but it had the reverse effect. If, after fifteen years, she had only just recalled a detail as sharp as that . . . what else might still be buried? Mightn't it be wiser to wait? . . . the place wouldn't run away, as her father used to say when she was too impatient.

No, *she* wouldn't run away either. She forced her legs to carry her up the stairs and through the main door. She thought the official on duty looked at her a little oddly. Ought she to give him some reason for being there? Say she was writing a novel about the 1914-18 period, needed some details of weapons and uniforms? No, that might lead to awkward questions. Or just say she worked in a publisher's and they were bringing out a book on the first world war . . . she was looking for an idea for the jacket? But would he believe her? And did she really work at a publisher's? She shut her eyes, trying in vain to envisage her proof-strewn desk. All she could see was a plate, with a little sepia picture stamped in the middle. It had been like a kind of reward, when one had scraped away the last of some horrid substance under their ruthless eyes, to see it there. It meant Tye had been a good girl. Not like the days Tye flung the plate, still nearly full, on the floor. Such peculiar plates. They didn't break, even though the floor was stone.

She gave the man a vague smile, then hurried

into the main hall. She couldn't remember anything like this. Perhaps the place was only a
museum after all and had never been anything
else. Feeling that a man in some kind of uniform,
with a spike moustache and a row of medals, was
watching her, she joined a group of schoolboys
and peered, as intently as they, at a large gun. Was
that man's face familiar? Probably just a type.
Uniform made people look alike. There'd been a
man in uniform at the door the day she left . . .
he'd asked her to give him some piece of paper.
. . . Anyway, it had been a different kind of
uniform. Perhaps they'd kept some of the male
staff on as museum keepers? She wouldn't of
course, know their faces; they had had no concern
with her. Yet hadn't there once been a man—just
for a moment, on their side—a man with a spiked
moustache?

She pulled herself together. If she was going to
get emotionally flurried and start fancying things,
she'd better walk out at once. No, that might
look bad, as if she felt compelled to prove she
could walk out. She'd come here to study the place
dispassionately, hadn't she? Forcing herself to
move slowly from glass case to glass case, staring
blankly at shells and aeroplane propellers, she
finally reached the end of the great hall, and finding herself alone, safely hidden behind a captured
Howitzer, she felt calm enough at last to look
around. This vast, high expanse, like the nave of a
church, belonged nowhere in her recollections.

The quarters she had inhabited must be somewhere away at the back. Perhaps they had been
pulled down. With a pang, half of relief, half of
disappointment, she realised that it was hardly
likely, in any case, that they would be on show to
the public. The hall was lit only from above; she
could not see any window through which she
could catch a glimpse of any part she knew. Then,
suddenly, in a bay behind a case in which, like a
corpse in an upright glass coffin, stood a life-size
figure in tin-hat, gas-mask, and mud-splashed
khaki, she saw a window. Edging round the
soldier as cautiously as if he were a sentry who
might challenge her, she looked through the pane.
And there, straight in front of her, was the
exercise yard, absolutely unchanged. She could
see the dark brown brick walls with their dingy
white stone coping just as she had always seen
them, as slabs hewn out of some giant wedding-
cake, almost petrified with age, like Miss
Havisham's. She knew every crack in the asphalt,
every broken slat in the bench that encircled the
solitary, sooty plane-tree in the centre of the
square. The yard was empty. But she felt, at any
minute, the door with the barred frosted-glass
panes in the wall opposite might open to one of
Patterson's keys and out would come the strag-
gling file. She had never learnt them all but she
could still sharply envisage the middle-aged
woman with the scarred face and the tall gipsy-
looking one who would have been handsome but

for those disfiguring yellow teeth, with long incisors like a wolf's. 'Old Nick' they called her, because she was always 'giving trouble.' Once she had sunk those yellow fangs in Roberts' wrist, and it had taken three people to over-power her in her fighting rage. After that, it was a long time before Old Nick reappeared in the yard. And there was the quiet little thing who never gave any 'trouble' at all, who looked like a prim, pretty schoolgirl and kept moving her lips as she walked, as if memorising her homework. Julia had always wondered how she came to be there, her fresh little face looked so strange among the others, mostly coarse, haggard or sallow. The rest she could see only as masks, set in a particular expression, sullen or blank or inordinately cheer-ful; one or two serene, almost saintlike.

She heard footsteps approaching. In panic, she clutched the window ledge, not daring to look round. What was she doing here, hiding behind a glass case? She must have slipped through some forbidden door. No wonder the yard was empty. They'd missed her from the queue and they wouldn't let the others out till they found her. Was it Roberts or Patterson coming to recapture her? She clutched the ledge tighter, head bowed, shoulders hunched, expecting a voice to say:

'Up to your tricks again, Tye? Any more non-sense, and you know where we'll put *you*.'

A voice did speak just behind her. It was man's and obviously not addressed to her. It was solicitously asking someone if they felt faint and would like a glass of water. Then a hand fell on her shoulder; she turned and almost screamed. She was facing the uniformed man with the grizzled moustache. Was he the museum keeper or the one they had fetched from the men's side to help overpower Old Nick? No, he was both men at once, just as she was two women at once. One this side of the window, in an admirably tailored suit; one out in the yard in a shapeless smock.

'Now, now . . .' someone was saying. That was how they always began—in that false, coaxing voice. In a desperate effort to escape, she dodged away from the glass case containing the soldier and took refuge behind another. Then she saw the figure standing deceptively still inside it: a uniformed nurse, staring fixedly at her and coldly smiling. Now she knew for certain where she was and who she was. She sagged down on her knees before the wax dummy, whimpering:

'No . . . Oh, no! . . . Not *there* . . . Not in the pads. . . . Don't put me back in the pads! . . . I'll be good, Nurse Roberts, I'll be good!'

ANTONIA WHITE

was born in London in 1899, and educated at the Convent of the Sacred Heart, Roehampton and St Paul's Girls' School, London. She trained as an actress at the Royal Academy of Dramatic Art, working for her living as a freelance copywriter and contributing short stories to a variety of magazines. In 1924 she joined the staff of W S Crawford as a copywriter, became Assistant Editor of *Life and Letters* in 1928, theatre critic of *Time and Tide* in 1934, and was the Fashion Editor of the *Daily Mirror* and then the *Sunday Pictorial* until the outbreak of the Second World War. During the war Antonia White worked first in the BBC and then in the French Section of the Political Intelligence Department of the Foreign Office.

Frost in May, her first novel, was published in 1933. The three novel sequel to that famous novel, *The Lost Traveller, The Sugar House* and *Beyond the Glass* followed between 1950 and 1954, forming a quartet in which Antonia White charted with extraordinary precision and intensity the growth to maturity of a young Catholic girl in the first decades of this century. Her only volume of short stories, *Strangers* was first published in 1954: this re-issue includes an uncollected short story 'Surprise Visit', first published in *Art and Literature* in 1964. She wrote one work of non-fiction, *The Hound and the Falcon,* an account of her re-conversion to the Catholic faith (1965). All of her works are published by Virago.

Antonia White translated over thirty novels from the French, most notably the works of Colette: her first translation, Maupassant's *Une Vie* won her the Clairouin Prize in 1950. Like Colette, Antonia White was devoted to cats and wrote two books about her own – *Minka and Curdy* and *Living with Minka and Curdy*. At one time married to H T Hopkinson, editor of *Picture Post,* and the mother of two daughters, Antonia White lived in London until her death in April 1980.